Threads of Amends

Threads
of
Amends
Mia Dorsch

Copyright

Copyright © 2023 by Mia Dorsch

Hardcover ISBN: 979-8-9916886-2-8
Paperback ISBN: 979-8-9916886-3-5

For all those who dream of something more than this world,
along with my mother who indulges me in my little fictional fantasy.

For those who think we're crazy, along with my brother and
father who find this concerning.

Table of Contents

Chapter 1:
The Sign

Sneaking out. My best ability. My hands instinctively push open my window, revealing a full moon rising above the black horizon. I grin as I hop up on my windowsill.

"Julius, you know this is a poor idea, do you not?" a voice questions me from behind.

I turn my head to him, rolling my eyes. "Whatever."

This boy is Soterios, a family friend's son. He is spending the night. I, on the other hand, am in the middle of leaving. He straightens his glasses and looks at me through the two glowing orbs on his face.

I look away. I won't listen to the likes of him. I let out a sigh and jump down to the roof below. My feet brush the shingles as I slide onto the ground. Soterios' watchful gaze pierces my back.

"Hey! Don't just stand there and watch me!" I snarl at him in a hushed voice, staring up at my bedroom window.

The glare of his glasses obscures his eyes.

I can only feel his gaze.

He frowns and closes the window. The lock clicks shut. His freckled face turns away as he leaves.

Man, that guy gets on my nerves.

Pumping my arms, I sprint through my parents' cornfield. The abyss of the crop engulfs me. My whole body flinches at the slightest sound. I can't let my parents catch me. I don't want to be seen by anyone I know, either. Other than *her*, of course. She's the girl I am going to visit. The tight corn maze feels endless. I weave through the stalks, expecting the end to be within the next few rows. To my dismay, it isn't. Once someone enters the corn, everything looks the same until they finally emerge from its relentless depths.

Corn isn't native to this world, which adds to its alluring, ethereal aura. The first cobs of this crop came from the Overworld, a parallel plane of existence to the Mirror Realm, my home. The Mirror Realm geographically resembles Earth. Other realms exist, but I know little to nothing about them. All of my knowledge about the Overworld comes from Soterios' family, who frequently travel from one realm to the other. I live in Vertrauville, which is the geographical equivalent of Germany. But slide the clock back a hundred or so years, and that's my village. Our farmers don't have combines or modern machinery. Commoners in the Overworld use 'phones' and other cellular devices, but residents here are centuries away from those technological developments. Soterios has a phone in the Overworld. I used it once, but prefer watching films on television whenever my mom and dad drag me along to visit his family.

I bite my lip, wondering what Soterios' motives are. His miserable voice haunts me. He speaks as if he knows everything. Well, he might, actually. He attends the Mirror Realm's most prestigious academy. His deliberate actions could be taken straight out of a school textbook. He couldn't act on a whim if he tried, though. Catch him off guard with a fight, and he'd cluelessly freeze. Still, adults love him because he's a little *snitch*. He tells parents everything they want to hear. Teachers as well, if I had to guess. Even if he's paid to do so, he can't keep a secret. He's quick to inform others about their wrongdoings and mistakes. I can only hope that he goes back to bed.

I stop.

Why was he in my room anyway? What a creep. It's not like him to be up in the middle of the night. What are the chances that he just happened to be wandering past? That doesn't even begin to explain why he was in *my* room. I am also extra cautious when it comes to making noise. How did he hear me? I shake it off and decide not to think about it. Back to my mission.

I bite my lip. A brisk gust of wind ruffles my auburn hair. I adore autumn. The howl of wind on chilly nights is like music to my ears, reminding me of my mother's whimsical wind chimes. I smile with nostalgia. I remember what a timid child Soterios was, hiding under blankets and furniture whenever the wind howled. He's still shy and reserved. Some people never change. As a child, I was very mischievous. That free spirit stayed with me into my teens. It's what inspires me to leap through windows and venture out at midnight.

I let out a large sigh of relief as the corn rows finally come to an end. A small strip of dirt stands between me and the woods. Lots of terrible things have been said to happen in this forest. I march into the multicolored foliage with confidence, knowing I have the power of mana on my side. As a skilled magic user, it takes a lot to intimidate me.

Not everyone is familiar with mana. The poor oblivious sheep. Mana is a magical energy that can be found inside people. Not everyone has it. Each mana user has a specific amount, sitting in them as potential energy. It can be converted to kinetic energy through the use of wands and chants. Of course, mana can replenish after use, but a magic-user's potential energy capacity never changes. My magical potential energy is nothing to turn a blind eye to. It's much more than average. Though higher

capacities exist, I have no right to complain. At least my mana capacity is better than Soterios'.

Like the corn, the trees of these woods engulf me in a world of their own. An ominous fog looms over the ground. The twisted trees' leaves flutter down to the ground, amongst a sea of their fallen comrades. Another thing I love about autumn is the colors. Shades of flaming reds, vibrant oranges, and glistening yellows fill the world. Though, their colors do not shine at night. They do not glimmer in this mangled forest.

I can't help but feel like I'm being watched. I slide my wand out of its holster. Holding a wand is similar to holding a pencil, we each have a dominant casting hand. Of course, like archery, as well, we have dominant aiming eyes. Mine are both on my right, so that's where my holster is, and where I hold my wand. Using a luminous spell, I light up the tip with a warm, golden light.

That's right. I use magic, Stalker.

People usually think that spells like this attract attackers. They do not. Using any type of magic can alert others that you can, and will, fight back with spells. When getting into 'wand fights,' you never know your opponent's spell set. That insensible factor deters many people from challenging anyone who has the power of mana on their side. The ability to change the colors of spells is another indicator of a user's fortitude. It costs extra energy to alter the appearance of spells. People with enough mana can craft a signature spell style. Usually, it consists of a symbolic color. I have only heard of this in a few cases.

Like with Mark Bruik.

That's the first person who comes to mind when I think of signature spell styles. His spells are purple, I heard. Rumor has it that his son is gifted with just as much mana, if not more. Apparently, Bruik is the headmaster of a school for magic. It's not the one Soterios attends. Bruik accepts anyone and everyone into his academy. How stupid. Magic schools should only accept the best and the brightest, in my opinion. Why waste your time on kids with low mana capacities and no work ethic? Even with his surprisingly average mana capacity, Soterios deserves to attend his school, as little as I want to admit the fact. He's earned his place by making the best use of his natural abilities. Plus, it'll lower a school's rating and ranking if they accept everyone. It makes no sense to me. If Bruik has the capacity to use signature spell styles, then he must be bright. Maybe he has an ulterior motive for his admission strategy. I hate people with unaltruistic underlying ambitions. They walk around knowing that everyone around them has been falling for an act.

"Julius." A voice interrupts my thoughts. I know that voice. It was *her* sister's.

"Happy to see me?" I release the spell but continue to keep my wand in my hand. I never know what she's up to.

"As if." She approaches me, emerging from the shadows. Her cold, dark gray eyes peer through me.

She can't use magic, but she has something called an ability. It's like a superpower. A mana user cannot have an ability. An ability user cannot have mana. People who don't have either can only hope for a charm to increase their power levels. A charm is a rare new power or trait gifted to an individual by a very powerful being. When charms were first explained to me, they sounded like a concept pulled from a folktale. After meeting a Charmed individual, I had to believe in them, along with omnipresent beings. Very powerful entities exist in this world. There's no doubt about it. Even gifted people like me avoid admitting the fact that we're at the mercy of such beings.

"Well, then. I'm overjoyed to see you, Melany."

Melany is a very fitting name for her. Of Greek origin, it means a person who is covered by shadows. That is precisely what her ability does. She can vanish into any shadow and remain unseen. She can sneak up on me at any point in time, as long as there's darkness looming around. I find it horrifying.

"Yeah, right. You're only interested in my sister." She jams her pointer finger into my chest. A chill runs up my spine. She's scary. Her black hair's sleek strands wave in the soft, midnight breeze. Her sharp nail digs into my skin. Surprisingly, I need to look up at her to see her face.

"That's enough, sister," a quiet voice says from behind. Melany grunts and crosses her arms. I spin around to find *her*.

"Lauralyn!" I exclaim and smile. She's my first real girlfriend. Before her, relationships never interested me. She became the exception. Because of her, I came to find that having a significant other isn't too bad. In fact, it's worth a lot of trouble.

Lauralyn has her sister's dark hair and fair skin, as well as her ability. Though she lacks Melany's height and aggression. We hug and exchange cheek kisses.

"If you need to sneak out every night to meet, why don't you just leave your family for good?" Melany pesters me. I stay silent. I don't have an answer to that. The idea never popped into my head before. This is, after all, my first relationship. My only reply is a shrug.

"The clan leader would not be happy if an outsider like him joined us," Lauralyn mumbles, rubbing her forearm. "Plus, he uses mana... none of the others would be happy with that."

I cringe a little. I tend to ignore the fact that Lauralyn has questionable connections. She and Melany are a part of a clan connected by their abilities. They reside in this forest. Usually, outsiders are killed on sight. That's why I come at night.

Sometimes I wonder if the clan is actually a cult. I don't know all the details, but they seem to worship a creepy entity. They claim it protects them. To me, it sounds like it strikes fear into them for their obedience.

"I don't like him, anyway. He's self-centered and annoying." Melany rolls her eyes.

"I'm right here, you know." I raise my hands.

"Do I look like I care?"

"Melany!" Lauralyn cries out.

"Someday *It* will give him what he deserves."

"*It*?" My eyebrows draw together.

"You know. Our deity."

"Deity!?"

"*It* wanders the woods of this realm. Scary, is it not? *It's* responsible for all curses and charms."

Curses. The opposite of charms. They're given in the same way but are not for the benefit of the receiver. Curses are punishments meant to harm or hinder the receiver.

Melany's nose scrunches. "We're being watched."

"Do you think... it's *It*?" Lauralyn's eyes widen in panic.

"What a boring name that is. Can't it be anything more interesting? More letters? More syllables? Just *It*. I would command more fear with a more fitting name." A deep, rusty voice fills the forest. The once-white fog turns black.

I gasp. Lauralyn wraps her arms around me and

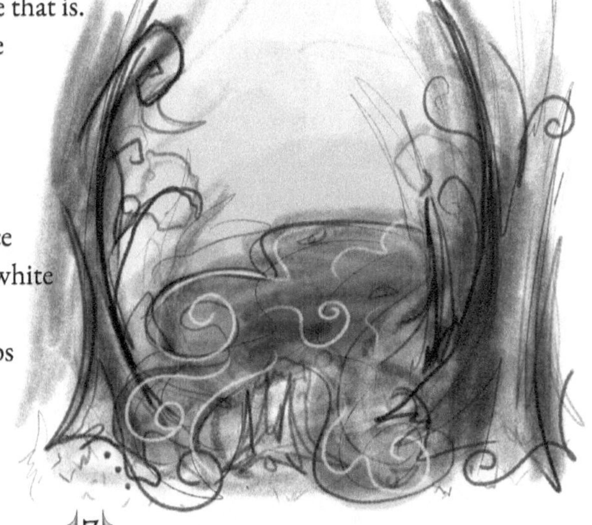

presses her face against the side of my chest. Her whole body quivers. My own chest shakily rises and falls.

"You want to join my people?"

"No!" I boldly reply. "Leave us alone!"

As I respond, Lauralyn slips out of my grasp, vanishing into the shadows from which she came.

"Aggressive, are you? I like that. Though, you have not answered my question."

My jaw drops. I have no interest in joining a cult, especially in these creepy woods. Plus, what would my parents think?

"I'll give you a count of three…"

"One."

I do not want to live in fear. No one does. I do not want to be ruled. I hated my parents for trying to contain my every action. Rules are meant to be broken!

"Two."

This thing will not want me to defy it. But I don't have an ability? I can't join the cult. I have no idea what to do. Think! Think! Think!

"Three!"

The lump in my throat grows. I can't even cry out, "No!" I don't want to join! I tighten my grip on my wand.

"Time's up!" It sings.

My throat feels as if it's closing in. I gasp for breath that I manage to catch, but I still feel as if I'm suffocating. The surface of my body tingles, pricking with an unknown, unpleasant sensation. Almost itchy, but too agitated to touch. With no other way to escape from my own skin, I collapse onto my knees, curling over. My strained fingers clutch my chest, pulling on the soft cotton fabric of my shirt. Melany smiles at me before vanishing like her sister.

Ruling with fear.

This was *It*'s wrath. This was *It*'s punishment for meddling with *It*'s cult. I reach out my hand to the sisters. Though they're out of sight, I know they're there. I want to scream for help, but no noise comes out of my mouth. I sense their backs turning to me.

What?

Why?

Is this betrayal?

It laughs.

"Oh, small boy. This world is so much bigger than you. I want you to see it. *All of it.*"

My eyes grow weary. My body grows heavy. My mind slows.

My eyes flinch. The morning light hurts my head. Everything looks like it's glitching. I blink hard as I push myself off of the ground. It hurts. The world is choppy. Did he take away my vision? I looked around. No, I can still make out the forest. Teal and bright red copies of what I am seeing tear reality apart. I cover my eyes in agony as I stagger through the trees.

I can hear *It*'s mechanical laughter somewhere in the distance. Whether it's in my mind or in this forest, it's there. I throw my first against a tree. The trunk shakes as leaves fall gently to the ground.

"You know this is a poor idea, do you not?"

Soterios' voice haunts me. I hate admitting it but, I should've listened to him. I should've listened to him. I— I— I—

"Punching trees will get you nowhere." I hear Soterios' voice.

"Eh?" He thinks I'm stupid, doesn't he?

"Did your hearing get damaged?"

"Hey! Don't taunt me!"

"I wasn't taunting you. I genuinely wanted to know." I can hear his circular glasses click against the bridge of his nose. I hate when he straightens his frames like that, so matter-of-fact and preppy.

"Did you follow me!?"

"When you weren't at breakfast, I got concerned. I used a tracking spell to find you."

It's that late already? My family always eats at eight o'clock. It would take a good hour or so for someone to venture this far into the woods. It must be mid-morning by now.

"Why?"

"We're friends, right?"

I begin to laugh. Friends? What is he thinking? What goes on inside of his crazy brain?

He keeps silent with his lips tightly sealed.

"For you to consider me a friend... Wow... That's sad. Do you even have friends? Acquaintances? Allies?" I snicker at his misfortune. I wonder if this is how his friends treat him in the Overworld, assuming that he has any.

"Are you trying to shame me?" His void of a voice questions me.

"Are you that blind? I knew you had vision problems but I didn't know they were this bad." Taunting him is irresistible. I am not one to resist temptations. I've been taunting him like this our entire lives, and each and every time, he still gives in.

"Look, Julius, I'm here to help you."

"Help me? Like you could do anything." I uncovered my face, keeping my eyes tightly shut. "You couldn't even hold your own in a fight."

"Do you intend to challenge me?"

"I wouldn't mind." I point my wand toward him. He gasps. I open my eyes to find him pulling out his wand in retaliation. His figure sways from side to side. Despite being on break, he's wearing the tan sweater, dark brown blazer, and matching pants that make up his school's uniform. A teal version and a red version of Soterios fade in and out of my view. My eyes sting. My brain can't take the stimuli. I open my mouth to shout a spell, but he beats me to it.

"*Éblouir.*"

Right. His French magic. Some say it's one of the most difficult magic-casting languages to learn.

The spell causes my vision to go white. I collapse on the ground yet again. I gave him too much time. When the effects of the spell go away, I find him holding out his hand to help me up.

"Your wand was pointed at a tree," he informs me. I try getting up on my own, but slip and fall back down. I flail my limbs in anguish, letting out a childish yelp of displeasure.

"You have my apologies if I hurt you. That spell is not meant to inflict pain on the opponent."

"I don't want your apologies." I put my hands over my eyes once more. "I–I just want—I want you to go away!"

Soterios holds his tongue.

"Let me help you." His voice remains stern. He knows I'm in a vulnerable place of weakness. I turn my head away and grab his hand. It's soft like a child's, free from manual labor and true hardships. His arm shakes as he struggles to pull me up. "What happened?"

"Do you believe in deities?"

"No."

I sigh.

I'm going to sound like a delusional idiot, aren't I? Though, what other choice do I have?

The wind makes our conversation bitterly brisk. I rub my hands together as I explain what had happened. I should've worn a jacket. I only have on my standard sneaking-out attire: a gray t-shirt, casual brown pants, and hiking boots. After telling him what happened, I hang my head low, waiting for Soterios to list my faults.

"It sounds like a hallucination to me. Were you drugged, perhaps?"

I shake my head. There's no way. Unless Melany's nails were poisoned. I doubt the idea. She already has an ability, so it's not possible that she has a venomous superpower. Soterios has a very objective mind, though he acknowledges magic and 'mythical' creatures exist. The Overworld raises children who seek logical and scientific explanations for all events. I bet he even believes in the Big Bang theory and the laws Sir Isaac Newt, or whatever his name is, came up with. But will he ever believe me?

"This reminds me of a being rumored to inhabit these woods—"

"You mean *It*?"

"Yes, that was the entity's name. A textbook stated that researchers of the past that *It* has a cult of worshippers that have existed for millennia and speculated that *It* has god-like powers and the ability to curse and charm anyone. Though, *It* could not take those curses back. A single, greater being has to do that."

Back at it again with the walking encyclopedia.

It dawns upon me. Lauralyn and Melany are both a part of the cult. Maybe *It* does not want me to join *It's* cult. Maybe I invaded *It's* territory one too many times. Then why did *It* not kick me out before? Why did the sisters not kick me out for *It*? Why did *It* ask me if I wanted to join?

"So you believe in them?" I'm surprised to hear his knowledge of this supposed deity and its followers.

"No. This is only what I have heard. Judging by the state you are in, you were probably poisoned. Certain potions are able to compromise a person's eyesight. Victims can either tough it out or find an antidote."

"But what if I'm not just injured. What if I'm actually cursed?"

"That would be the worst-case scenario. If that were true, we would need to find the greater entity. I doubt that it is possible."

Rumors say that there is a female god-like figure somewhere in this world. She has the power to create and destroy worlds at her will. Everyone is at her disposal. *It* apparently was a failed creation of hers. One that acted out of spite and was controlled by pure malice. If It acts out of malice, then why would it charm people? Maybe one story is wrong. The information I have is entirely crafted out of gossip and folklore, so it cannot be fully trusted. As someone born to two very religious parents, I try to refuse giving into such pagan fables.

"Or," he thinks for a moment, "you can learn how to properly utilize it. Charms and curses are raw power. Still, it is probably poison."

He is most likely right, but I don't want to believe him.

"Maybe. I can't stop thinking about the black fog, though."

Something about the fog, the voice, the cult, and the strange sensations isn't sitting right with me.

"Going back home is the best option right now." I hear the click of his glasses yet again. "Adults will know what to do."

I beg to differ.

"No!" I shout.

Going home like this would be the worst option. My parents will pity and punish me. I *will* fix this before I see them again.

Soterios sighs. "There's a town not too far away."

"Let's go there. Anywhere but these woods." I begin to walk forward but run face-first into a tree. Out of surprise, my eyelids

pop open. My eyes sting in retaliation. I dig my fingers into their sockets to suppress the pain. Never again do I want to see anything. I get up on my own this time and brush myself off.

"Put your arm around my shoulder," Soterios instructs me. I feel him brush my side. I grunt and begrudgingly put my right arm around his shoulders. He's taller than me, so I have to reach up. After all, he comes from a family of very big people. He has a slim build and is about five foot nine. From what I heard, he's not biologically related to them. Maybe growing up around tall people made him a giant as well.

He turns around and begins to lead us toward our next destination. I try my best to match his speed and not stumble over my own feet.

"The way you speak bugs me," I say out of the blue.

"It does?" His tone shows no sign of offense.

"Yeah. You're so monotone. It's deathly boring."

He apathetically shrugs his shoulders.

"Nevermind that. We've got company."

"What?" I raise a brow.

"Two girls with black hair."

I gulp.

"Just who do you think you are?" I hear Melany inquire. Her voice alone chills me. Soterios shows no signs of being intimidated by her.

"Soterios Solace."

I grunt. He's always so literal and upfront. Even oblivious, at times. I almost feel bad for him. I can't imagine what it's like living in his shoes. How humiliating it must be.

"And what do you think you are doing?" Melany goes on.

I do not reply.

"I'm afraid you're in our way," Soterios states.

"Oh, you want to play that game," Melany snarls. Her footsteps grow closer.

"I appreciate the offer, but I am not interested in games."

I can't believe what he's saying. He's trying to get us both killed! I keep silent. To be honest, I'm curious to see how this will play out without my intervention.

"You're the one who's playing games!" Lauralyn aggressively retorts. I never knew she could get mad. She was always so calm around me. I scowl. Was it an act? Is this who she really is? A ferocious cult member who worships an evil deity of spite?

That's it.

"Don't mess with us!" I draw my wand and blindly point it around.

"I thought *It* taught you a lesson about coming into our woods, our territory!" Melany yells. Honestly, there were a lot of warning signs. Lauralyn was always so timid and cautious around me. Melany constantly gave me death threats and declared things about her clan's territory. Did I listen? No.

If only I saw this coming...

"We're trying to leave."

If Soterios is trying to be polite, it's not working. And it's not going to work, either. I sense Melany lunching at us.

"Attack!" I yell.

At the same time, Soterios exclaims, "*Arrêter*!"

I hear a loud snap. My eyes grow wide.

"What did you do?!"

"I used a binding spell to detain her."

"Melany!" Lauralyn cries out. I sincerely wish to help her but I know she is no longer on my side. Tiny tears well up in my eyes. Oh, how quickly my first romance ended. Maybe I have a poor taste in girls. Back to the matter at hand.

"The spell won't last much longer. We need to go." Soterios tugs on my arm and begins to run. His sprint is more like a jog. I scramble to catch up. He pants. Running is not his strong suit. Even when we were little, I always beat him during races. I easily keep up with him.

"Watch out, there's a branch."

"A wha—?"

A thorn-covered branch slaps my face. He could've warned me sooner. After recovering from that incident, we continue our escape.

Soterios slides out of my grasp. He has a terrible coughing fit. I can't do anything but blindly stand above him. This cardiovascular fiasco is entirely his fault, though. If he was active and athletic, he wouldn't be having this problem. His choice to find me in the woods led to this as well.

I slightly open my eyes and peer down at Soterios, who is curled up, clutching his stomach. I tightly shut my eyes after a moment.

"She stabbed me," he mumbles.

"What? When?"

"During the spell."

"Who?"

"The short one." My teeth grit together. Does she really want to get rid of me that badly? Alas, I once believed there was something special between us. I should've taken the time to get to know her. Soterios grunts as he stands back up. His hand latches onto my shoulder. "I fear that she rubbed poison on the blade."

I clench my fists. She always told me how she could handle attacks. She had shown me that knife before. She told me it would teach anyone who messed with her or the clan a lesson. What effect does it have, though? I place my hand on my chin, trying to remember.

Aha! That's it!

"She told me that the knife is coated in a poison that will make you extremely sick if you're not treated. It's used to make sure the clan's enemies die a slow and painful death."

"I see."

"You're not scared at all?"

This guy is unbelievable. If I were in his position, I would be freaking out. He never fails to surprise me.

"No. You said it can be treated. A town is just up ahead." Soterios coughs some more before he grabs my hand and pulls my arm back over his shoulders. His unsteady hands shake.

Chapter 2:
The Medic

We head into town. As always, the town bustles, never skipping a beat. Footsteps and chatter surround us. The aroma of fresh-baked bread from a bakery fills my nose. I could be enjoying this more if Soterios wasn't coughing every so often. He turns a corner and leads me down a few different roads. From the sounds and smells, I can tell we are in Medenelle, the city of trade and bargains. I know a couple of teens around town and we have some family friends here as well. The plan is to find James, one of my friends who works at his mother's pharmacy.

Soterios comes to a stop. I hear his knuckles make contact with a door.

"Come in," a voice calls out. A small bell rings as Soterios swings open the door. We walk inside. My eyes flutter open and shut to find that we're in the pharmacy. A boy greets us, his thick black hair covering his eyes. He wears a dark gray sweater with blue stripes, as well as a matching scarf. "What can we do for you?"

Before either of us is able to reply, the boy speaks again. "Oh! Julius! It's you. What in the world did you get yourself into? It looks like you just came out of a grave!"

"*Yooo*, Reo." I hold my fist out for a fist bump. His hard knuckles smash into mine. Typical Reo. "Life is cruel, as usual. You?"

"Ah, not bad, not bad. Business and sales are booming. What will solve your current, *uhm*, problems? And this guy, his problems, too?" He motions towards Soterios.

"We're looking for a medicine or antidote for Soterios." I point to him with my free hand.

"Do I look like a doctor to you? I'm a fashion designer! I'll go grab James. He'll have this under control in no time."

Soterios coughs into his sleeve.

"Antidote, eh?" Reo mumbles before yelling, "James! Julius is here, ya bum! Get over here and—"

"I get it already." Footsteps approach us.

James Thomas. Unlike most people in this world who use magic, he is an ability-user. Abilities are said to be genetic mutations. His ability allows him to create ice at will, even on a hot summer day. The material he is able to manifest is more powerful and sturdy than ice created using magic. The consequence of using his ability is that he gets frostbite. Yikes.

Reo, on the other hand, is what many residents in the Mirror Realm call a normie. He has no special powers. No ability. No mana. No curse. No charm. He's just...Reo. His fashion brand is known throughout a few realms. Without a doubt, he's very talented and extremely cre-ative. His hairstyle reflects his unique creativity. I can't imagine being his poor barber.

"Who's that?" I feel Reo pointing to Soterios. He always points. Every time he does, someone tells him it's rude, yet he still points at people and things whenever he gets the chance.

"I am Soterios Solace."

"Holy heck, man. That's a nasty wound."

"A cult member stabbed me with a poisoned knife."

"Right to the point, I see."

Despite being in a technologically delayed world, I hear James snap on latex gloves. Modern medicine and medical instruments are usually seen in the Overworld. That's where they all were invented. I wonder how he imported his gloves, but don't bother to question him. He and Reo, despite residing in different realms, are cousins. His family has strange ways of getting supplies despite being horrendously dysfunctional. I can only assume that Reo's family provides medical instruments for James' family. Most of the Mirror Realm's medical practitioners focus on utilizing natural treatments with sources found in this world and healing spells. Though, spells do not cure all wounds and ailments, especially if the caster is not well-versed with illnesses. Some magic users dedicate their whole lives to perfecting their understanding of medical magic and curing the sick by utilizing mana.

"Come here," James demands. Soterios wiggles himself out of my grip.

I battle the distorted blur of my vision to sit down on a stool next to Reo.

A few minutes after James takes Soterios into another room, Reo pipes up, "You two look close. Are y'all in a relationship or something? Did you run away from your parents' disapproval?"

"No. Of course not. There's nothing to like about him."

"If you say so. You haven't opened your eyes since you got here. What's up? Am I really that hard to look at? You could've said so."

"Soterios told me I was probably poisoned like him. I think it's a curse."

"A curse, eh? Don't tell me you actually messed with the cult in the woods."

"I did happen to have a relationship with one of the members," I admitted sheepishly.

"*Ugh*, you're an idiot. You most definitely got cursed. Did you get Medusa powers or something? Laser eyes?"

"I-I'm not sure. Whenever I open my eyes, the whole world glitches. It stings."

"Huh, that's odd. Could you open your eyes for me? Just for a moment."

I nod and do so. I have no idea how Reo examines me through his dark hair. After getting too close to my face for a little bit too long, he leans back and sighs. I shut my eyes, grateful for the relief.

"Everything looks normal to me. As I said, I'm not a doctor. I'm not a magic nerd, either. Back to your friend. Who is he?"

"He's not really my friend. Our families are close. We've just known each other for a really long time."

"Aw, that's sweet. You came here of all places for treatment?"

"Soterios brought me here after I told him about James. I'm basically blind right now. Luckily, when we got out of the woods, we ended up on the outskirts of Medenelle."

"Speaking of Medenelle, you know this is the city of trade, right? Nothing is free around here. Especially medical services. Do you—"

"Reo, profits aren't everything." James walks back into the main parlor of the business. Only his footsteps approach. Soterios must be in an examination room. I bite the inside of my cheek. I hope he's alright. Much to my chagrin, I can't help but worry about him.

"It'll be fine," James assures me. "This poison is only dangerous when it goes untreated for a long period of time. I've dealt with those who have escaped the cult many times. It would be foolish of me to not keep the antidote on hand. He might have a nasty cough for a few hours, though. I cleaned the wound and put in a couple of stitches."

I let out a sigh of relief. "Thank you, James."

"You have gotten us out of poor predicaments in the past. This is the least I could do for that boy."

James is a very nice guy around companions, but when faced with strangers, he's very cold. I hate that he trusts me enough to be comfortable and open around Soterios. It took years for James to open up to me, so I'm jealous that he quickly welcomed Soterios. Not many people get to see this side of him. All I can do is smile and enjoy this nice side of James while it lasts.

"Yo, James. Could I ask something of you?" Reo suddenly requests.

"*Will you pay me*?" James mocks Reo, who takes his words to heart. He can be cruel to his family members from time to time. He isn't on the best terms with his mom, and his dad isn't in their family's picture.

"Of course, man. Could you examine Julius' eyes for me?"

"That's a strange request? Why?"

"We think he got cursed."

"Oh, really? Follow me down the hall."

I cringe. I can either blindly run into everything in my path or brave the stinging sensation and open my eyes. I take it like a man. James leads me down the hall and into a room. We pass a few doors, one of which I'm assuming Soterios is behind. My crooked vision almost throws me off balance.

"Care to explain?" James inquires.

He gestures for me to sit down on a cushioned bench. I nod and tell him about the events between last night and this morning. James listens intently.

"Ah, I see. Just look at this."

I open my eyes and find his hand in front of my face, along with

the white sleeve of his lab coat. The teal moves upwards. A light blue latex glove covers his palm. His hand slowly follows close behind, leaving a trail of red. The teal moves right. His hand moves right. The red moves right. The teal moves left. His hand moves left. The red moves left. The teal moves down. His hand moves down. The red moves down. Everything stops. The teal and red move everywhere. They radiate off of his hand as it struggles to stay perfectly still in midair.

"I know what the curse is!" I proclaim, placing my hands over my face. I dig the bones of my palms into my eye sockets to take away the searing pain.

"You do? Haha, that was fast. I thought it was my job to diagnose. Looks like Reo doesn't owe me after all."

"It has something to do with predicting the things that will happen."

"Oh? You really see the future?"

"*Mhm.* Only a little bit into the future, though. Enough to screw up how the present looks." I cross my arms.

"That can end up being helpful if you learn how to use the visions to your advantage."

Footsteps pound down the hall. The door creaks open, probably just enough for Reo to poke his head inside.

"James! Are you finished yet? It's lunchtime! And I'm hungry."

"Ok, ok. Can you go out and pick something up? I'm clearly busy at the moment."

"Geez. I see how it is. I hate doing work. I'll leave the hard tasks to you since social interactions are not your strong suit anyway." Reo trots back towards the entrance. I hear the door's bell ring before it slams shut.

James searches through a few drawers as he mutters small insults under his breath. I raise an eyebrow. His nimble hands shuffle through clutter until he finds what he's looking for.

"Lean forward."

I follow his command. I feel something wrap around my head. A blindfold.

"This is so you don't need to worry about accidentally hurting yourself or straining your eyes."

I thank him.

"Will you be staying for lunch?"

"Oh? It would be a sin to pass up that offer." A grin grows across my face. I realize I haven't eaten since dinner last night.

I'm grateful for James' medical assistance and hospitality. Though, I'm not sure if I should tell him my plans just yet.

"So, you're probably not going to go home until you're all fixed up."

Darn it. He knows me too well. I'm not easily ashamed of myself, but if I returned to my parents like this, my dignity would never recover.

I play it off with a chuckle. "You guessed it."

A few hours later, the bell rings, announcing Reo's return to the pharmacy. The door slams yet again.

"*Hey*! I got a huge pot of chili from Granny's Chili Pot. It's the new hot spot around town!"

James and I had been waiting on the stools in the parlor for him. I hear Reo set a heavy item on the table. I hear the clamor of utensils and porcelain dishes. Honestly, out of all the times I've visited James here, I always thought that his china set was merely for decoration.

"Aren't those only for special occasions?" I ask.

"We have guests. It's not every day that we all sit down like this for a meal," James replies.

"Oh, Julius is still here. Is the glasses guy still here as well?" Reo squawks. "Guess we'll have to split this chili four ways."

Soterios? Does he not remember his name? What an idiot. I can't expect any more of him. Soterios is out of sight in a treatment room. James told me he needed rest right now. We'll deliver a meal to him later, or give one to him if he comes out.

"Did you figure out anything about the curse?"

James and I explain what we discovered.

"Oh, so you just need to learn how to use it." Reo plops a few ladle-fulls of chili into three bowls.

"I guess so." One warm serving slides into my accepting hands.

"If you can see further into the future, that would be very useful," Reo says with his mouth full of food. It is obviously too hot for him.

"Dangerous, if you ask me." To cool his chili down, James blows on it. "It's a curse, after all."

"Curses and charms are the same things." That dull voice I hate echoes down the hall. My eyes widen under my blindfold. "The only difference is how it affects the receiver. Both are raw energy bound to living beings. It is the person's choice to determine what they do with it." Obviously, Soterios has to add his knowledge to the conversation, even from behind a closed door.

"So this curse could turn into a charm if he learned how to use it properly, eh?" I can almost hear Reo smirk.

"Precisely. In order to do that, you must find a powerful magic user, or expert, to help you," Soterios states as the door hinges creak open. His footsteps approach us.

Yet again, Mark Bruik is the first person who comes to mind. He's a headmaster, so he wouldn't have the time for me during the school year. Either way, I still don't trust him. Soterios' academy operates on a different schedule, which is why I'll be stuck with him for the next week.

"I heard of an alleged magic genius who lives in Milledale's forests. We should see if he's willing to help," James suggests. "His name is Zacharias. Someone was discussing how he sparked others' interests in researching charms."

"Isn't Milledale kinda far?" Reo complains. "*Argh*, my tongue feels so dry."

"You burned it on the chili." Soterios is back to his normal, straightforward self, I guess. I shove a spoonful of chili into my mouth. The flavorful foreign food is new to me. It's probably from the Overworld.

Reo offers him a bowl, which he politely accepts.

"Are your eyes any better now?" Soterios asks.

I shake my head. "No, but at least we have good food."

"My mother is very good at making chili," Soterios adds. He doesn't gag, so he must like it.

Reo gasps. "Is she the owner of Granny's Chili Pot!?"

"No, she is not."

"Speaking of that, what did you give Granny in return for her food?" James skeptically interrogates Reo.

"Coupons." Reo jams an extra large spoonful of chili into his mouth, having learned no lessons. "For my fashion business, don't worry, James. I won't take away from your profits. Well, maybe I told her you'd be happy to help her at a low price if she ever burns herself."

A mere miracle manages to keep all the chili inside of his mouth as he speaks.

"Back to Zacharias. How will we get to Milledale? And how will we find him once we get there?" I ask.

"If we hurry, we can take the sunset train. It'll take us to a neighboring kingdom. From there, we can walk and find him on foot," James replies.

"We need a lot of planning for that. The sunset train takes an overnight trip to arrive at its destination." Soterios tells us. "In addition, Milledale has acres upon acres of forests. Finding a singular person would—"

"Eh, we'll be fine. Maybe someone knows him." Reo shrugs.

"I always have a travel bag packed for occasions like this."

Reo scrapes chili out of the bottom of his bowl. "Time to get packing."

His footsteps depart from the parlor.

"Why don't you take a seat?" James offers to Soterios. "We can plan without Reo."

"Who needs plans? We can just wing it." I finish my bowl of chili and set it down in front of me.

"We don't know what Milledale will be like, so there's no use in putting any plans in place." James sighs. "Reo will want us to treat him like royalty, if I had to guess. He goes on million-dollar vacations, so all we need to do is prepare for his petty attitude."

That's the problem with normies. They can't do anything for themselves. They get dragged along on adventures and aren't able to do a thing about it, just like rag dolls. Still, they demand respect and attention. Neither I nor Soterios reply. His logical brain and occasional helplessness remind me of normies, though he can clearly use magic. After all, he attends the Mirror Realm's top school for spellcasting.

In Reo's world, Overworld dwellers see him as a successful young man. Here in the Mirror Realm, his accomplishments mean little to nothing, if anything at all. Since he can't fight, he's just another mouth to feed. Staying alive is a more difficult feat here. People like him are usually forced to learn combat skills or are sold as slaves for labor. His family, like Soterios', primarily resides in the Overworld, so if anything like that was to happen to him, he could always get pulled back and provided with protection there. On the other hand, James' family lives here in the Mirror Realm. His mother lives upstairs, above the pharmacy, and his father is a wanderer that doesn't contribute anything to the family business. James and Reo are cousins, so the two spend a lot of time visiting each other despite being native to different realms. I thank my lucky stars that I'm not blood-related to Soterios.

"Mother!" James calls out. "My friends and I are taking a trip! Can you tend to the pharmacy while I'm away?!"

Something falls on the ground upstairs. He takes that as a yes.

"Also, we have chili! You can have some when you wake up!!"

"She's asleep?" I ask.

"That's my mom for you. She'll sleep until she absolutely *needs* to get things done. Soterios, you should get more rest, too."

He says, "I'm fine," before coughing a few times.

Reo finishes packing up and we prepare to leave for the train.

"Heads up!" James throws a satchel at Soterios. Somehow, he manages to catch it. "It zips at the top. You'll be in charge of our food supplies."

"Okay," Soterios obediently replies. "Is it refrigerated or filled with non-perishables?"

"Just snacks. We can buy meals."

He also tosses a jacket my way, which I immediately put on. He tells me that I'll catch a cold from wearing short sleeves in this weather.

"Do you have Milledale's currency?" Soterios asks.

"What do they use?" Reo comes back with another question.

"Gold, silver, and bronze coins."

"What's he? A travel guide?" Reo laughs. "Don't worry, I probably have those somewhere in my lavish wallet. We can always barter with coupons, anyway."

"Not every kingdom is like this city. How do you even make a profit, Reo?"

"I overprice everything. The best price, that I still profit from, can be obtained by using coupons. How do you get those? You help me in some way or give me something. Like with Granny's chili."

James groans, but I chuckle. Neither of us thinks that she is going to be utilizing her fashion coupons anytime soon.

"You gotta give me credit. It's a splendid idea. That's how I pad my wallet."

"Isn't your family already wealthy?" I pester him.

"Yeah, they live in New York City. They are the richest of the rich. They own an art foundation you know. Guess who will be their successor?!"

"Oh, so your parents live in the Overworld, too." Soterios' voice is smaller than usual as he ignores Reo's ridiculous rhetorical question.

"Ayy! Maybe I'm not the only normie here. Hey, wait a minute. How do you know so much about the Mirror Realm then?"

"I attend school here."

"Reo, can't you tell? The uniform he's wearing has *the* academy's crest on it. On top of that, normies are not able to attend it. I applied, but because I'm an ability user, I got rejected."

"Yikes, that sucks, James. Where do you attend school?"

"I work more than learn. Well, learning medical skills is my work right now. Very rarely do I attend classes. Just math and literature when I feel like it at the community learning center."

James has a bright mind. He doesn't need to take any more than that. His mother teaches him science and medicinal skills at home when she's awake. He knows how to properly brew potions and is familiar with a vast range of herbs and magical ingredients.

"If we keep chatting, we will miss the train."

"Right." I stand up.

Sometimes, I am very grateful for Soterios' sense of responsibility and lack of a filter. Not too thankful.

As we were heading out the door, Reo asks, "*James*, can you carry my bags?"

"Seriously? Why? No way."

I feel someone grab my hand. "I wanna be the one to help Julius. We can't have him blindly fall into the filthy dirt road!?"

James rejects Reo's request. He must now carry his own bags while assisting me.

"Why am I getting the feeling that I probably shouldn't trust you?" His hands latch onto mine and yank me to my feet. "Oh, right. That's because I *don't*."

I rest my case. Putting my life in the hands of Reo is a big mistake. Can he even see with his ridiculous hair covering his eyes!?

"I have a great idea," Reo announces. "We can try getting a blind discount for Julius. After all, he can't see very well. Illegally blind, if you ask me. He and I can go buy train tickets while you wait down the line. Then, you can latch onto the train and—"

"Isn't that fraud?" Soterios asks.

"I'm not blind and you will *not* tell anyone that I am."

James does not respond. As kind and gracious as he is to me, he isn't a, quote on quote, 'people-person.' What about being surrounded by strangers doesn't he like? I have no idea. He makes himself scary and cold in public to push others away. At least, that's my hypothesis. I suppose it's only natural for him to be cold. After all, he has the ability to create ice.

"Let's do it."

My jaw drops.

"I'll hop on the back if you save me a seat."

He what!?

At the ticket booth, Reo covers up the bottom of his face with his designer scarf and tries acting like my father. We're clearly not related and he can't possibly pass as my father with his height. Even though I'm vertically challenged, I have a good two inches or so on him. Soterios is supposed to be a relative of ours. He's even taller. I'm pretty sure that we're not going to fool anyone.

"Why, hello there, kind sir." Reo makes his voice as deep and rusty as possible. His voice is naturally low, so his father impression

is somewhat believable. "I'd like to buy tickets for me and my sons."

"Would you like your own car?"

"Oh? Yes. Yes, please. How much will it increase the price?"

"In comparison to what?"

"Four—I mean three tickets."

After raising a brow, the clerk replies, "It'll be about double the price, though you will have ample space."

Sleeping in a chair sounds awful. I hope Reo takes that into consideration.

Reo clicks his tongue. "Yeah, we'll take it."

The price shocks me. Reo willingly pays up in coins and coupons. "The coupons are for the most fashionable business this realm has ever seen."

There go all of his life savings, I can't help but think.

"Your car will be the caboose."

Reo cheered. "Yes! Best car!"

"You're not actually a father, are you?"

"How dare you say that! Come, children!"

Reo curses and insults the salesman the moment we turn our backs on him. I suck my lips in and hope that poor man would not associate the words that carelessly roll off of Reo's tongue with the rest of us. I'm only grateful that the clerk didn't ask us any more questions.

We make it onto the train station's waiting platform, and Reo latches onto my arm. If any one of us was a father, it would most definitely not be him. He's a clingy, spoiled child. I know I talk a lot of trash about people, but that's truly him. Raised under his parent's wing, he thinks he can do anything and everything. The worst part is that he doesn't accept the repercussions of his actions and always finds a way to wiggle out of punishments.

"Reo, your acting skills need improvement," Soterios critiques Reo, who gawks.

"Wow. Thank you very much. We got our train tickets. That's all we need. But uh, hopefully, James knows where to hop on."

"Keep your voice down." I scold him, not wanting anyone else to find out.

"Right! Oops, I'll be quieter."

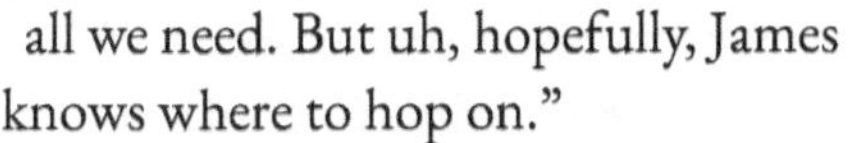

The sounds of shuffling feet and chatting townspeople fill the station. An employee shouts, informing us that the train will be arriving shortly. Minutes later, we get word that the train will be running very late.

The other passengers around us grumble and check their watches. Rail travel isn't cheap, so their frustration is understandable.

The delayed train arrives, and we shuffle into our car. Since it's the caboose, we're at the far end of the platform. Reo had already finished all of our packed snacks in the two hours that we waited. Despite the effectiveness of the antidote, Soterios still had a cough. Unlike many places in the Overworld, the Mirror Realm's transportation has no sense of urgency. As the three of us board the train, the conductor checks our tickets. Steam from the locomotive disturbs my lungs. Thanks to being the only passengers in the caboose, we don't have to push and shove for a spot.

"To the back, to the back, to the back!" Reo drops his bags and sprints to the back of a car, as his chanting implies. I push my blindfold up on my forehead to see what's going on. I can make out bunk beds on either side of the car. Soterios shoots me a worrisome glance. I close my eyes. If something bad was going to happen, I didn't want to see it.

The train whistle bellows and the car lurches forward.

"It's his time!" Reo shoves the back door of the car open. I hear the metal groan.

"He's really doing it..." Soterios' footsteps make their way out of the rear door.

"Grab my hand!" Reo cheers. I orient myself to the space around me with my hands and join Reo on the back deck. The rumbling train speeds up with each passing second. James, who is preparing to hop on the back of the train, rushes to catch up. His breaths grow heavy as Reo desperately chants his name. His hand claps with Reo's. I open my eyes to catch a glimpse of James hoisting himself up, onto the caboose's platform. If I truly am able to see the future, I can say that he isn't going to fall back onto the tracks. I shut my eyes in relief, pulling my blindfold down.

"James! Guess what?"

Still panting, he grunts in response.

"It turns out we have the whole caboose to ourselves. You didn't need to pull that snazzy stunt back there."

James sighs before shoving his way into the car. He flops right onto one of the bunks, making it creak under his weight. James has a decent build. I'm willing to bet it's because he's always running some sort of errand for his lazy mother, whether it's delivering prescriptions or yanking herbs out of the forest. If anything, he has more muscle mass than free time.

Reo pulls me back into the caboose before continuing to nag James. "*Hey*, I wanted that bed!"

James makes no effort to appease Reo. I haven't seen him out of the pharmacy since we were children. His mother happens to be the same way. As a doctor, she cares deeply for her patients, yet as a mother and as a woman, she doesn't give a rat's rear about her son or anyone else. I never wonder why his father left. I don't think anyone else questions it either. From time to time, I wonder if James will leave when he's no longer legally dependent on her.

Reo argues with James in vain for the next few minutes. Soterios keeps to himself, on the bed above mine.

"Don't speak unless you're spoken to." I pick up his nearly inaudible words that gently glide through the air.

I recognize the phrase. Where from? I rack my brain, trying to figure it out. Right! His teacher scolded him once at his fifth-grade graduation, which I was forced to attend. Poking him with her wand, she said those exact words.

"What a kind thing to tell yourself," I sarcastically grumble with an eye roll.

Soterios' breath pauses for a moment after a deep inhale. I can almost sense his fingers curling, as they always do when he feels pressured. More like when he is under pressure. I'm never truly sure if he *feels* anything. He just analyzes everything, like a robot. He bases his thoughts on the data he collects, I bet. The things others tell him rewire his brain like a computer.

"It's none of your concern. Are you alright with that bunk?" Soterios' voice now calls down from above me.

"Oh, whatever. It's fine."

"Okay. The view is nice from up here."

"Eh? That's the first subjective opinion I've heard from you."

"Sorry. After the sun sets, I'll go to sleep."

"It's that astounding, huh?" The urge to see out of the window wells up within me. After all, this train *is* named after the stunning daily phenomenon.

Soterios pauses for a moment before mumbling, "Yes."

Envy gets the best of me. If the sunset is enough to evoke Soterios' opinion, it must be bewildering.

"*Gyah*, I can't take this curse anymore! I just want to see normal again!"

I tear my blindfold off.

The golden cornfields whizz by as a flaming orb sinks below them. Its burning colors bleed across the horizon, giving way to nightfall. I dig my fingers into my eye sockets. The beautiful scenery plays over and over again in my head as if it burned itself into my brain.

Then it strikes me that I saw everything clearly out of the window. With enough, focus, I'm able to control my visual input, but a few moments are all I can take. I also notice that Reo and James finally shut their mouths. Their bickering always gets on my nerves.

"Are you seeing what I'm seeing? That cloud resembles a heart!" Reo cheerfully chirps.

James lazily grumbles.

"It must be a sign." Reo snickers.

"Ew, gross," I interject, sticking my tongue out. My first love ended in brutal betrayal. I flop on my side, knowing that the best thing I can do right now is sleep.

My dreams are strange. They feel so real. In one, I am a teacher at Bruik's school, which is the last place I'd want to work, spending my future working for that shady guy. I just can't place my finger on what about Bruik I can't trust. In this dream, a horned boy finds his way into my unusual workplace, demanding that I help him. He is a lot like me. Young. Arrogant. Narrow-Minded. For some reason, in the world of the dream, I harbor none of those traits, as if I grew out of my naive tendencies.

Is this... a glimpse of the future?

I wake up, my forehead coated in a cold sweat. Only the rumble of the train riding across the rails can be heard. No light peeks through the edges of my blindfold. I guess it is around three in the morning. Some call it the witching hour, mostly because that's when freakish monsters emerge from the dark depths of night. Others believe that is when hauntings happen. As a child, I always hated the early morning hours. Only the most unfortunate individuals experience the horrors of waking up at three in the morning.

I let out a grand sigh and rest my hand on my forehead.

"Are you awake?" a quiet voice asks.

A ghost!?

Panicking, I quickly reply, "No."

"So you are..." The voice belongs to Soterios, the last person I want to talk to. Even after Armageddon, if we happen to be the last people on the face of this realm, I will still dread communicating with him. "Would you mind if I came down? I haven't been able to sleep for hours."

"Hours, eh?" I raise my brows.

"Yes. I woke up at midnight. It's now three thirty-two." I hear him slide off of the top bunk. That's right, he wears a digital watch but keeps it hidden under his uniform's sleeve to avoid drawing any unnecessary attention. The bed by my feet sinks down. "Do you think they can hear us?"

I take a moment to reply. Reo is known for his deep sleep. I could dump him in an ice bath and he would still be sound asleep.

James, on the other hand, snores like there's no tomorrow. His snoring almost makes Soterios' subdued speech inaudible.

"No, they can't."

"Okay. Good. Do you hate me?"

"Do I what?" I suddenly sit up. His question disturbs me.

"Hate me." His words are clear and crisp. He told me about a public speaking class he took in the past. His diction and enunciation are far better than that of others our age.

"I—"

"Be honest."

"Yes."

He sighs. "I knew it was a worthless question."

"I-I did...hate you. But I do owe you, after all, you saved me back there."

Soterios keeps silent. His breathing is unsteady, almost as faulty as someone who is about to cry. I always get this lump in the back of my throat that disturbs my breath before I sob.

"It's worthless, right? Removing myself from opinions and hiding any signs of emotions?"

"Huh?"

"Nobody at my school accepts it, either. I thought that if...I didn't express myself...if I didn't...have differing opinions...that maybe..." He pauses to take a deep breath in.. "...people would like me."

"I'm not going to lie, that's stupid. You should be able to be who you want to be. If someone doesn't accept your feelings, then you know what? Screw them!" I whisper-scold him. He gasps.

"Thank you. I'll work on it."

I smiled slightly. I wonder if he is smiling too.

Fortunately, he changes the subject. He never dwells on emotional topics for very long. "Do you think the cafe car is open?"

"Oh, I hope so."

The weight lifted from the edge of the bed. "Want me to bring you something back?"

"How about an iced coffee to jumpstart my morning? Extra sugar. Whipped cream. Sprinkles, if they offer them. I'm obviously not going back to sleep."

Surprisingly, I get some light rest before Soterios comes back.

"Jumping from one car to another is a difficult task, especially with one's hands full."

"Tell me about it." I roll my eyes and sit up.

"You really slept with no blankets?"

"*Mmmmmm*, maybe," I cross my legs and adjusted my posture. "I was too lazy to put them on."

Soterios places a drink in my hands. It takes a moment for my palms to adjust to the cold surface.

"It doesn't have a lid, so be careful," Soterios informs me. "It's better when there's a top, especially when driving cars. Or when you're blindfolded."

A joke from Soterios? I think. Though, I'm more interested in his other statement.

"You drive?"

We don't have cars in the Mirror Realm. I've only seen them on trips to the Overworld with my family.

"I can't legally drive on roads without a license, but my parents need me to shuttle items from the front of our property to the back in our family's pick-up truck."

"Oh, wow." I never expected Soterios to skirt the law. Nor did I ever realize how many surprises he hides.

"I'm rather fortunate. Most of my classmates will never get to ride in a car, let alone drive one."

"Unless the Overworld's culture continues to influence ours. Just like this train. It's imported." I take the first sip of my drink. Ironically, the sugary overload calms my senses. Cream coats my lips, like too much lipstick on a woman. "Also, this stuff is delicious. Thanks."

"Oh, good. Apparently, the train's staff work around the clock."

"*Yikes.* I'll put this on my eternally growing list of places not to work."

"Speaking of that, what would be the ideal profession for you? Clearly not serving on a train."

I shrug as I swirl the iced coffee around with my straw. "Dunno. What about you?"

He takes a few moments to brainstorm his answer before he finally replies, "My teachers tell me I'd be fit for an office job. They said administrators are always in high demand at the academy."

"What do *you* want to do?"

His response takes a little longer. "Write books." He pauses before adding clarification. "Textbooks."

I raise my brows. "Wow. Fascinating." I chuckle quietly at my own sarcasm. "I guess textbooks always need to be updated. Sounds boring if you ask me, though."

"Precisely, but I do not mind. I would like to uncover new information or history about unknown locations. Writing novels or academic journals about such information sounds appealing."

"Then do that," I tell him.

"Can you two be quiet?" James grumbles in his sleep, rolling over to face away from us.

I snicker. "Go back to bed."

"I will."

"I smell something nice. Whatcha got?" Reo's bed creaks.

"Noneya." I grin.

"Noneya...what?"

"Noneya business."

"Julius, you jerk."

"If you would like something, you can always take a trip down to the cafe car," Soterios interjects. Calm and blunt, as always.

"Ah, uh, about that, how did you pay for what you got?" My eye twitches as the realization hits me.

"I told them a joke."

"A joke? Really? You're not even funny, Soterios." Reo mocks him.

"Yes. They were bored when I came in, so when I asked them what they wanted, they told me a good joke, so I gave them one in return," Soterios explains. "I then told them a few stories about the Overworld and my travels. We shared the conversation over a few cups of tea until their shift ended."

"I would say we should totally meet up in the Overworld someday, but you're such a bore. Those poor workers probably ended their shifts early because of you." Reo seems to have picked up how easy it is to poke fun at Soterios.

Soterios sighs. "They were intrigued, actually. It's easy to take for granted the fact that we have ties to the Overworld, along with this one, Reo. Few people here understand phones, cars, or any of the Overworld's technology. Trains and boats are the closest this realm gets to modern civilization."

"Oh, boy. You're chatty today. Must've been all that tea. You know what sucks?" Reo complains. I raise my eyebrows. Soterios shakes his head. "You reminded me that data doesn't work here."

"I bet we could find an internet connection spell," I add, grinning.

Soterios reminds me that we would need electricity to run cellular devices, so my spell idea gets shut down.

"Hey! Check out that sunrise!" I can't keep up with Reo's scattered brain.

I lift my blindfold up at his suggestion and glance out of the window. The world glitches. I squint in agitation. The world goes back to normal. My mouth sits ajar in perplexed triumph as I tear the blindfold off, tossing it to the side.

"Eh!? James fixed you up with that under my command!" Reo cries out. "Are you cured now or something?"

In a hushed voice, Soterios questions me, "With enough focus, you can control the curse, can't you?"

"He can—what now? So we didn't need to come on this stupid train to find that crazy magic man," Reo interjects.

I bite the side of my cheek and avoid eye contact.

"If he wishes to use this curse as a charm, we must find him," Soterios stands up for me.

Reo puffs his cheeks out with a prompt *humph*. "How come everyone else around me gets cool, strong abilities but I don't!?"

"Be glad..." James states, his rusty voice muffled by his pillow.

"Says you, the man who can create ice."

"Having an ability requires immense responsibility."

"That's something you could not handle," Soterios adds.

"I'm older than all of you! I'm a legal adult in my country! I–I–" Reo's lips quiver as his eyebrows frown. He gasps for enough breath to wail, "I could handle it!"

Soterios slightly gasps. I know what he is thinking. Reo feels younger than us all. I am not surprised by his age. For an adult, he sure is immature. He doesn't like being left out. He has 'F.O.M.O.,' as people usually label it. Fear of missing out. The only thing he accepts criticism on is his brand and fashion designs. Even with those critiques, you'd really need to have a phenomenal point in order to get through to him.

"That's enough," James demands. His deep voice startles me. Reo obediently stops yelling.

Soterios spends most of the morning reading. Reo and James take their time getting breakfast from the cafe car. I impatiently wait for them. My blindfold sits tied above my eyes while my hands are folded in my lap.

"That book can't possibly be that thrilling," I murmur.

"It's neither here nor there. Comme ci, comme ça. The plot is nothing unique, yet the writing is honorable. It is clear that the author dedicated a lot of time to their craft. The artist worked hard as well. The illustrations throughout the novel are sights to behold."

"If the plot is bad, then why are you reading it?"

I hear the click of a pen.

"Analysis."

"Voluntary or for school."

Soterios sighs. "Voluntary."

I grimace. People who annotate books need a life. "Geez. Is it also in French or something?"

"I am far from fluent, so no. The plot takes place in France."

"Oh, so it's about the Overworld."

"Yes. A fictional mafia there, in fact. It's about friendship and betrayal. Secrets, too."

"This doesn't sound like your cup of tea."

"Sometimes it's nice... a break from nonfiction works... I can live a fulfilling life through the eyes of another—"

"French person," I continue his sentence.

Soterios ignores me and gets back to reading. I pick at my nails out of boredom. I begin to wonder what in this realm Reo and James are up to. Getting breakfast can't possibly take this long. My stomach grumbles.

"We should have asked them to bring something back for us."

"I might have some money in my pockets."

"Oh? Really? Why didn't you pay before?"

"Mhm. They didn't request anything. Mother always advised that it's a good habit to keep currency prepared in case of an emergency. Reo's ideology of exchanging coupons for goods is actually genius."

The muffled noise of Soterios sifting through pockets fills the car in our voices' absence. The train galloping over the rails rests under all of our movements. Deep in my core, I can feel us shifting in time and space. Our caboose feels still, but the world outside rushes by without fail.

Soterios hops down from his bunk. He leaves me with a quick, "I'll be back."

Hopefully, he's done with jokes and storytelling so he'll be back sooner rather than later. I kick back and relax. The repetitive rattle of the train soothes my mind, almost making me drowsy. I remember when we were kids, Soterios loved the railway. He and his family dragged me on many adventures to train stations just so he could sit and watch them whizz by. We'd wait for a couple of minutes or for hours to see one come through. I pretended I didn't like it, but the Overworld's trains were so much more advanced than the ones we have here in the Mirror Realm. They shot past like bullets. As children, after extra fast ones passed, we'd sit there dazed with bewildered eyes and wind-blown hair.

Reo and James return first. Reo moans and complains about eating too much. James ignores his comment and walks right past me to the back of the car. The rear door creaks open as his boots make contact with the deck's steel plates. Reo taunts him about potentially falling off.

James' silence, though common in public, feels unusual.

I catch him mumbling about wondering where his father was. The life of a free-spirited traveler is so foreign to us. Soterios and I know three places, my farm town in the Mirror Realm, his rural neighborhood in the Overworld, and the train station, which we haven't been to in years. Well, maybe he knows four, if I include his academy.

I wonder if this is the furthest I've ventured from home, from safe, well-known land. The space between me and my family's farm grows with each passing second. I brush off the thought of our parents searching for Soterios and me. My mom would be crying out my name through subtle sobs. Soterios' mother would hold onto her hand, offering comforting words. Despite the fact that she and Soterios are not bound by blood, she holds a deep love for her adopted son. Many aren't aware of their situation, both his mother and her husband have brown hair and freckles like Soterios, so he blends in with their family. I wonder if they knew he'd end up looking similar to them.

Soterios returns with two warm, flaky pastries topped with bread crumbles and seeds. Their savory aroma makes my stomach plead for food. He sets them each on a cloth napkin before giving one to me and keeping the other for himself. After quickly

thanking him, I bite into the fresh pastry. Cheese filling pours into my mouth. Just what type of gourmet chefs do they have in the snack car? I may never know, but I don't exactly care if I find out or not. The taste is far more than enough. I wolf down the rest, but still remember to savor each and every scrumptious bite. I think about complimenting his choice, but reconsider.

After my snack, I take a nap. The horned boy comes back to my dreams. He has matured since the last encounter. He is entangled in a battle against a boy adorned in purple robes. The two draw their swords. The handle of the sword belonging to the horned boy has been wrapped with gauze. Its tattered strands support his hand. The others' blade has a refined aura, yet the noble wielder still holds back. Behind the feuding duo, a man, around thirty years of age, peers at them from the comfort of his throne. He doesn't care about the boys' sword fight, nor for the two youths' safety. It's almost as if he wanted them to battle. A dark crown of shadows encircles his brow while a red cape lays draped over his back. Punishments for the encouragement of such violence never seem to come. Sparks fly up, down, left, and right as the two silver swords clash. The noble boy in purple draws back, lamenting in an unknown language.

The times seem to change.

The boy he once sparred with stands by his side, the two both bruised and scarred from battle. I hate to think that they're probably my age.

"*Sic semper tyrannis.*"

Deep in my subconsciousness, I feel that he's talking about the ominous man on the throne. The horned boy spreads the Latin saying. He stands alongside troops on the frontlines. I almost feel sympathy for him. I never worried about war or the dangers of battle, but the two were responsible for fighting something, for *saving* something.

I never find out if the duo succeeds.

When I wake up, I discover that I am crying. I rub the tears from my eyes, unable to recall the rest of my dream. My mind blurs with both delusion and reality, fogged with contradicting thoughts. Reo tells me that our stop, the end of the line, is approaching.

Chapter 3:
The Path

The Sunset Train only has two stops, Medenelle and Pericuton, leaving us only one place to disembark. Fully awake and blindfolded once more, I wait in the doorway for my companions to finish collecting their belongings. Reo shoves me through it without a warning. James, our stowaway, sheepishly rushes past the conductor, avoiding eye contact. I thank the conductor who extends his hand to help me jump down. He checks our tickets and skeptically looks over his shoulder before turning us loose into the city of Pericuton. I have heard mixed reviews about the place, having never been here myself. Some people claim Pericuton is dangerous because of its quarrelsome history, but others appreciate its past value. It is said that part of the village had survived countless wars and centuries of weathering. I had seen the distinguished architecture and notable marble pillars from looking at artists' past renditions. Reo, continuing to act as my guide, hustles me through the station. From the sound of our clambering footsteps, I can tell that the floorboards are made out of wood. The damp hardwood sinks slightly beneath our boots. The moist air smells of recent rain. Reo compliments the fine fashion choices of civilians as we enter the village. As he describes their attire, I conclude that the commoners in this part of town must have expendable money. I assume, since this is a port city, many people here are international traders. The soft sound of waves lapping against the shore catches my attention as salty air fills my nostrils. Our group traverses the stone brick streets. Soterios and James both keep to themselves, occasionally murmuring or making observational remarks. To be honest, they would make good friends. Both have a vast knowledge of magic, herbs, and other things I pay little to no attention to. Both are probably too reserved to open themselves up to the possibility of companionship. I brush the thought off, keeping in mind that Soterios is a loner for a reason. Horns and sailors' calls from boats echo through the streets. The fresh, salty scent fades into a stark, fishy smell as we continue our walk through the coastal village. I usually hear that port cities always have a shady side. Many illegal trades and treaties get signed in these places. With my thumb, I raise my blindfold to take a peek at our surroundings. That, and I can't shake off the feeling that we're being watched.

The people scowl at me. Many have scars, tattoos, and prosthetic limbs. Even the children have twisted frowns and ragged clothes. They seem very different from what Reo described earlier. No one appears to have their eyes set on our group. A blacksmith files down blades and sends sparks flying all over his workplace. Street performers flaunt their absurd instruments and strange talents in order to make quick pocket change. I pull my thumb away. Reo jeeringly whistles despite the intimidating townsfolk around us. He stops to ask someone for directions.

"Hey, you! Which way is Millidale?"

"Ya wanna follow that trail over there, it'll be sure to take ya to Millidale. Beware of gangs. Many, *many* folks will try'n steal your treasures." The old man jitters as he speaks.

"Thanks, dude. We'll be fine."

In the Overworld's films, any time someone tells others that they will survive or be alright, the opposite ends up happening. I groan, knowing the words 'we'll be fine' quite frankly seal our fate.

We will be anything *but* fine. Thankfully, we don't have any valuables on us, other than Reo's coupons, if they even count. Reo drags me in the direction of the trail. Though I usually avoid taking strolls and hikes, stretching my legs feels nice, even if it means I blindly follow where Reo leads.

I can feel the moment the pavement disappears as my feet sink into soft mud. The watery ground growls and gurgles under the pressure of our boots. Reo pauses. I continue forward. He declares that he will not, by any means, walk in the mire and that someone must carry him. James takes on that responsibility, carrying the childish adult on his shoulder. I pull my blindfold off to catch a glimpse of the shifting evergreen trees, and, of course, to become my own guide. I squint, trying to force the shifting images to return to one. To my surprise, they do.

With a triumphant *hmph*, I march down the sloppy path, shoving my blindfold into my pocket. As long as I can keep my vision focused, I won't be needing it anymore! I tease Reo by running ahead, kicking up the soggy dirt.

"Ooh, look! A little dirt don't hurt!" I chimed. "City boy!"

I pick up a handful of the mush and fling it at him.

"Hey!" He squirms out of James' grasp. He stumbles to his feet and chases after me.

We must have been running for miles. Thankfully, we stop for a breather. I bet Soterios needs it more than me. Still, my lungs burn as I grip my knees with my hands. Reo flops over by a bush. Mud covers his matching sweater and scarf. James sighs and shakes his head at us. Brown smudges accent his white lab coat, but in a bad way. Soterios waits for us to collect ourselves, his face buried in his book. What a drag, as always. I'm tempted to muddy his book, but I have a little respect for literature. Enough to keep me from ruining it, at least. Maybe it was because of my mother. She loves novels and would read me children's books every night before bed until I turned ten. I begged her to read to me after that, but she told me that I was old enough to read on my own. To me, it's never the same when I read alone. That's why I don't pick up books anymore.

"Should we leave him there?" I gesture to Reo. James shakes his head. Soterios has his face buried too far in his book to comprehend and respond.

"*Noo*! Don't leave *meeee*!" Reo's babyish whining starts back up again and continues as we carry on with the journey. A howling wind rushes through the thick, dark trees. Pine needles stick to Reo's already filthy scarf and sweater. Mud splatters my pants and jacket. Somehow, Soterios looks almost untouched.

"Don't you have a cleaning spell or something?" Reo picks debris off of himself and plucks leaves out of his matted hair.

"You wish. Even if I did, I wouldn't use it on you," I retort.

"A magic user, *hm*?" An unfamiliar woman's voice taunts us from behind. "I should've guessed that by now."

We turn around to find a masked lady approaching. She tightly grasps a greatsword in her left hand. A duo of hooded attackers waits behind her. I reach for my wand, curling my fingertips around the handle.

"Only those gifted with powers have the luxury of such privileges!" she sneers. Her amber eyes burn with the flaming rage of envy. Her red lips curl. "Walking around so boastfully, viewing the sunset from that train, enjoying an easygoing life!"

"Where did that come from?" I grumble, glancing over at James. He makes eye contact with me. She must have been the one watching us in Pericuton. My gaze returns to the woman. Jealousy indefinitely has ways of getting under people's skin. I, of all people, have envy issues. I was always angry when Soterios knew a spell that I didn't and absolutely furious when he could cast my favorite spells better than me. I'm still that way now, but at the same time, I'm glad that I didn't trade a social life for magical expertise like he did.

"You know the ill will those without abilities feel towards us. Even Reo gets petty about it," James whispers.

"Surely, you have something of value. Something worth my time." She narrows her eyes, pointing her sword at me. I aim my wand back at the woman. Both Soterios and James have their focus locked on her hooded subordinates. Knowing his powerless position, Reo lets out a shrill yelp before backing away. He might as well be a lamb to the slaughter. He can't even wield a sword.

I cast the first spell, exclaiming, "*Acus!*"

An array of luminous white bullets manifest around the tip of my wand. With a flick of my wrist, I send them spiraling toward the woman, who deflects a few of the projectiles with her greatsword. A few poke holes in her cloak and rebound off of her silver chest plate. One of the ricocheting projectiles incinerates a few strands of my clay-colored hair.

Phew! That was close!

Right, the one thing my spell can't penetrate is metal. She tightens her grip around the handle of her weapon, readying herself to attack.

"I can handle her," Soterios mutters, stepping forward as he draws his wand.

"We shouldn't hurt anyone," James commands.

"What are you going to do, *run away*?" Reo mocks James.

James holds out his arm and curls his fingers. The strain of trying to produce ice causes his whole arm to tremble. Frozen crystals form around one of the henchman's legs, spreading closer and closer to his torso. He is quickly being frozen in place. James' ability can turn battles in his favor by immobilizing his opponent, not to mention the pain of impending frostbite.

Thanks to James, the three of us are now facing two remaining foes. Three because Reo is both helpless and useless in battle.

James extends his other arm, spreading his frosty fingers out. Spikes of ice rise from the ground around the woman's feet, but she swiftly dodges. His pin-pointed gaze gives his next moves away. With each attack, more and more snow crystals form on his hand, gnawing away at his fingers, palm, and wrist.

Soterios finally enters the scuffle, and casts a spell aimed at the fierce woman, who pays little to no mind to her frozen comrade. "*Vous Voyez!*"

She murmurs little curses of spite under her breath. Her irises bounce from one place to another, as if she is tracking multiple moving targets. Her red lips spread apart, into a scowl of gritting teeth. She slashes the invisible targets with her sword.

The seemingly spell expires when the woman charges toward Soterios, landing a hit across his chest. He would be sliced in two if he hadn't instinctively stepped back. Instead, he's left with a deep gash across his uniform and chest. I cast a binding spell, the same one that Soterios used against the girls in the forest, at the remaining henchman. Even though I don't mainly use French magic, I can cast a few spells with it. His limbs draw together as he falls to the ground, stiff as a board.

"You would be nothing without a wand! Not even a human shield," the woman insults Soterios, who staggers back. He presses his hand against his wound, pulling it away with a palm covered in

blood. My eye twitches. Only *I* can taunt him! I run over to provide him with backup.

Before Soterios can consider casting another spell, the savage woman slaps Soterios' wand out of his hand. In retaliation, Soterios places his fingertips together and utters a chant I know too well. A raw spell. Enough raw power to overwhelm a man's body and reduce him to ashes. I cry out his name. Shoving him to the ground, I beg for him to stop. His glossy eyes stare into mine as he stops to catch his breath. I let out a small sigh of relief, he did not finish casting the raw spell. Still, blood rolls down his forehead and soaks his sweater. My fingers scrunch the cloth of his sweater as I fight the tears aching to pour from my eyes.

I struggle to form the words, but I manage to wheeze, "*Somnum!*"

Slumber consuming her, the woman falls to her knees before passing out on the ground, her limbs sprawled out like roadkill.

"I guess I was going to die either way," Soterios face twitches, a small smile dawning upon his typically expressionless face. The pool of blood grows, soaking his uniform.

I helplessly kneel beside him, choking on thin air. Reo stares at us. James keeps his back to the scene. I shakily check his pulse. He isn't dead, but he definitely won't survive with the blood pouring out of his wound.

Suddenly, a figure haughtily approaches from the depths of the forest. His long strides seem composed, but are also quick with a time-sensitive purpose. Anyone knows who he is by his ghostly pale skin and scarlet eyes. After all, he takes the leading role in many folktales about blood-sucking beasts.

Vylad.

King of the vampires.

The first fanged human.

As if repelled by a magnet of the same pole, I instinctively rise to my feet and back away from the humanoid beast. The sleeping spell expires. The female assassin awakes. Taking notice of Vylad, she backs away, swiftly escorting her two incompetent henchmen out of the forest. If only I could have the same easy escape as them, but instead I must this cursed beast.

Vylad runs his thumb against one of his fangs. A wound opens on his timeless finger. Scarlet liquid rises up to the wound's surface and floods the little laceration.

"Do you want to be saved?" he asks Soterios.

Soterios stays silent, his eyes just barely open.

Vylad crouches down and examines my comrade. "You're a bright boy, buddy," he addresses me. "You stopped your friend from using forbidden magic that would have surely killed him. You'll understand what I'm about to do."

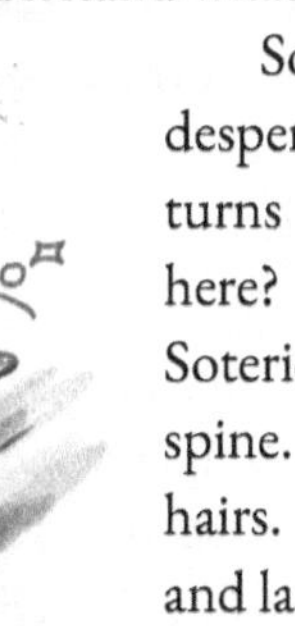

Soterios' lifeless gray irises glance up at me in desperation. I have no *clue*. Worst case scenario, he turns Soterios into a vampire. Why is he even here? He has nothing to do with our affairs. Soterios' distressed gaze shoots a chill up my spine. My skin begins to crawl under my raised hairs. On my way to help him. I slip in the mud and land on my rear.

I flounder to right myself wailing, "D—don't touch him!"

"Too late."

Chapter 4:
The Festival

Vylad lets the excess blood roll off of his thumb into Soterios' mouth. The nonconsensual patient sits up after the first few drops and clutches his throat. Vylad stands up and quickly licks his wound, which should be closing by now if he uses his vampiric healing abilities. Reo jerks his head back, appalled by Vylad.

"Some fashion statement," he rudely comments. "Also, that's gross. Like, just, ew."

To be honest, Vylad's striped sleeves under his black t-shirt is definitely a unique look. In addition, he wears torn, dark gray jeans with silver chains hanging out of one pocket. It's as if someone stripped his body and clothing of all colors. Not even his cheeks display traces of pink pigment.

"Welcome to the Mirror Realm! Enjoy your stay between the tangled threads of fate and magic!" Vylad puts up a peace sign with his fingers, his sharpened black nails poking up from behind his pale flesh. Reo merely stares back at him, too bewildered to craft a response.

My chest rises and falls. Reo's sass is going to get him killed, if not by Vylad, then whatever fairytale foe he insults next. On the contrary, Soterios could now be called an 'undead being' by simple-minded commoners who listened to tall tales, rather than facts. Overworld dwellers make up folk stories about vampires, like Count Dracula. To be honest, I never bothered to look too far into such traditional epics from that realm. People often mistake vampires for revived creatures, but they are indeed living beings. They're a whole cursed race, to be exact. When people consume the blood of vampires, they become one themselves. It doesn't matter if the act is forced or voluntary, they lose their humanity either way. I heard the curse spreads through blood, tainting the body of the recipient. Soterios becoming a vampire will surely become a wrench in our plan.

"It's better than being dead, is it not, Julius?" His blood red eyes glance over in my direction, as if they can read my mind like a book. Soterios puts a hand on his knee as he forces himself off of the ground. To his dismay, he falls right back. I can see skin trying to stretch back over his wound. Vampires' regeneration abilities are quite horrifying. They seem almost impossible to kill.

"Wait, what?" Reo looks from me to Vylad to Soterios, then to me again.

"Don't worry about it, kid, your friend is just a vampire now." Vylad gives Reo an enthusiastic thumbs up, along with one of his signature toothy smiles.

"Really? That was fast."

"Yes, I am the original curse bearer, so naturally, I know how long the process takes. I have extensive experience with performing this ritual."

"Will he be allergic to garlic?" Reo's naivete is enough to catch a monster off guard.

Vylad raises a confused brow. "Uh, no? I don't like garlic, though."

"Woah, seriously? That sucks for you. I love garlic bread so, so, so much. Can I be a vampire too?"

Vylad laughs at him before promptly responding, "In your dreams."

Soterios lowers his head, squinting. "Why would anyone *want* to be a vampire?"

"To not die, in your case. I couldn't help but save this poor, dying youth." He proudly runs his hand through his sleek black hair. "We're a cursed race, meaning that technically we're a charmed one, too." He winks. "I've looked like this for centuries because of it."

"Woah, so you're immortal? Soterios, you better be thankful for that!" Reo turns his attention from Vylad, to Soterios, and then back to Vylad. "And you don't show age!? Who wouldn't wanna be young forever?"

James turns to face us. "Didn't you ever hear that fairy tale about immortals?"

Ah, right. In exchange for longevity, immortals are generally misunderstood and forced to live a life of solitude. They lack relation to the common folk, and in vampires' case, they're feared by nearly every other living being.

"There are two sides to every coin. I personally don't let myself die because it's my responsibility to look over my people." He places a hand on the left side of his chest. "Our tragic fates were born from my faults."

At least he admits it. If I were him, I wouldn't have ever spread my curse in the first place. Plus, it's straight-up inconsiderate to forcefully share your atrocious fate with innocents. What a jerk move.

"But vampires are indeed mortal creatures." Soterios glances over at Vylad. "Vampires can only exceed an average human's lifespan by consuming blood. This peckish desire scares others away."

"You speak as if you're not one yourself, kiddo. How old are you anyway?"

"Fifteen."

"Aww, sweet little baby. You could be as old as me someday. Wouldn't that be fun?"

"No, I don't plan on it."

"*Hmph*, what a wasted opportunity." Reo puffs his cheeks out and faces away from Soterios.

"It's complicated. This is enough for now." Standing up, I step in. My voice is clearly unstable, my vision is as well. My head spins around in circles, too dizzy for my mind to fully grasp the severity of the situation. Vylad catches onto my fear. His pearly fangs reveal themselves as he grins.

"How can you accept this, Soterios!?"

He flatly looks at me before glancing off to the side. "With this curse, everything I've ever lived for is at stake. My family. My education. My future. This hopeless sense of helplessness is too much for me right now." His voice doesn't even shake. If anything, he sounds resigned to this reality.

"I say it's best to hide it and carry on." James rejoins the group as well. A veil of gloss coats his red and swollen eyes. His optimistic advice is in stark contrast to his questionable demeanor.

Was he...crying?

Soterios nods along to the awful advice.

"Continue your journey, young adventurers. Keep calm as your friends' wound heals itself. Remember," he sings, "he would have died without *my* help." Vylad salutes us and prances off into the woods from which he came.

"Hey!" I yell, chasing after him. My feet suddenly grow cold as I freeze in place. I look down at my feet, which James has engulfed in ice. My teeth grit together as I watch Vylad jeeringly stride away.

"Is something wrong, James?" Soterios asks.

He doesn't reply.

"Haven't you heard? He can't deal with death," Reo blurts out.

"Don't worry, James. I'm not dead."

"You do *look* pretty dead! We should find some place where we can clean up. I am in *dire* need of a bubble bath with my rubber ducks!" Reo crosses his arms, observing Soterios. He really does look like a corpse. Blood stains his clothes, covers his arms, and even runs down his face. Dark circles rest beneath his fatigued eyes. Even though his sweater has a gaping hole, the skin on his chest appears as unscathed where the wound once was.

Soterios thanks him with a hint of sarcasm before swiftly covering his eyes and slamming his head back to the ground.

I call out his name.

"Symptoms of vampiric transformations..." Soterios utters. "One...general pain. Two...fever. T-three...the desire to..." He stops.

"The desire to consume blood." James finished the list. "We have three days before he kills us all."

"Kills!?" I gasp.

"In movies, vampires always go bonkers without blood," Reo adds. "It's only natural."

"I've seen this affliction in the clinic." James sighs. "It never ends well."

"Hey, don't be morbid," Reo gawks.

In spite of our currently alarming developments, we decide to keep moving and go to the nearest town, which turns out to be the capital city of Milledale. James mentions a local inn called The Fae's Stay. Apparently, James and his father had met the innkeeper years ago, but even though he doesn't remember his face, James assures us that he'd recognize the innkeeper due to his unique aura. I wonder if it's similar to his traveling father's. That free spirit energy rarely goes under the radar.

Our motley, mangled group must be quite a sight. James carries the sickly Soterios over his shoulder. I hold his glasses so they don't fall and shatter. The last thing we want is for someone to be legally blind. After all, we have James and his frostbitten hands. Reo's poor attitude. Soterios' current circumstances. And, of course, my curse. Even though my vision is just fine, something feels off. Honestly, I wonder how our situation could get any worse.

We definitely stand out from others walking along the same street. Not only are they in good health, but they are also in good spirits. Some hang up floral garland while others craft colorful lanterns.

"Ooh, I wonder if they're going to host some sort of festival?" Reo prances to the front of the group. "It must be since I'm here!"

His inability to accurately read and respond to situations either lightens the mood or ruins it. The former applies to this scenario. Grateful for his oblivious contribution, I laugh at him.

James almost smiles.

"I bet it'll have great food." I grin, watching a young boy with tomato-red hair carry a bread basket across the street. "*Maaaa*! The buns are ready!"

A tall woman with long pointed ears takes the basket from him. A floppy hood gracefully covers her head in an attempt to cover her elven features. Other children who share his vibrant hair color stand around her. Some work while others play. A passerby on horseback smiles at the hardworking family. Horses are a common mode of transportation in the Mirror

Realm, along with unicorns and pegasi. Unicorns, like humans and elves, can use magic. They also tend to be smarter and more aware than normal horses. Pegasi are even harder to come by and are typically sought out by those with expendable income and the will to fly.

"These look splendid, thank you, Iggy." The mother smiles. I wonder if he's the favorite child.

"Iggy? What a horrible name," Reo mutters. "Sounds like piggy." I never understood Reo's need to make rude comments. James comes to a stop in front of a three-story building.

"This should be the place."

Sure enough, a sign hangs down above the doorway. 'The Fae's Stay' is carved into the side. The olive green and scarlet red paint have been chipped away from the years gone by. As we enter, the door's tiny jingle bell rings. A man looks up from the reception desk. The first thing I notice is the huge scar running along his face. He has the look of a seasoned traveler. His connection to James' father makes sense now. James was right about the innkeeper's aura. I gulp. I can't pinpoint why, but I feel intimidated.

The smell of salty appetizers fills my nostrils. The bottom layer of this inn must function as a tavern.

"Is anyone else starving? We should definitely eat here for dinner," I suggest, licking my lips. I'm suddenly aware of my growling stomach and the fact that we never had lunch.

"Oh, yes, totally." Reo casually waves to the rugged man.

"Kidnapping someone, I see?" The innkeeper crosses his muscular arms. "Aren't you a little too young to commit to a life of crime? Just look at your bunch." He laughs. "No matter what you're here for, what'll it be?"

"One night please," I request.

"Form of payment?"

"Do you accept jokes or storytelling?"

The man just chuckles. "If I'm in a good mood, maybe. You're from that trading town, right?"

"How did you know?" Reo's eyes widen. "I spend a bunch of time there."

"One, your accent. Two, look, that city is the only one with modern medical equipment, he's wearing whatever doctors wear these days. Scrubbles? Whatever they're called."

"Scrubs." James corrects him.

"Yep, those. You're Thomas' son, right?"

"Yes, sir."

"Then your room is on me. Your father has gotten me out of many tight spots in the past. He stopped by just a few days ago, as a matter of fact. It's a shame you weren't able to see him."

A tiny smile emerges from James' stone-cold face. "I haven't seen him since my eleventh birthday party. I'm happy he has at least one close friend."

"It should be his obligation as a father to visit you. It's a shame that he is a better adventurer than he is a dad. Looking back, I remember when you were just a lad and your father was still around. You were so young and carefree. I hear your mother has been working you really hard. I don't know what mess you're in now, but it must be better than working that sweatshop with her." The man pulls out a key and sets it on the wooden surface of the counter. A tag is tied to it, reading Room 3C. "Third floor. Third room."

"Thanks." Reo and I both reach for the key. I snatch it before he can and victoriously snicker.

"Meals are always free for guests," the man adds, glancing over at the eating area.

A good handful of villagers and voyagers eat at wooden tables and a polished bar. A man dressed in formal attire serves the myriad of guests, spanning from large families, to romantic couples, all the

way to adventurers with maps littering the table. Candle-lit chandeliers give the tavern a warm aura. The other side of the inn has a staircase and a common area. An old woman sits, knitting an ugly sweater. For some reason, she sits at the piano, rather than on the sofa. Reo opens his mouth to insult the poor lady, but I speak first.

"If you claim a table for us, we'll drop off our bags in the room," I tell Reo, who nods in compliance and thankfully goes in the other direction. Acting as his filter is a full-time job. No wonder James is always tired of him.

Soterios still hanging off of James' shoulder, we climb the narrow staircase and make our way down the candle-lit hallway to our room. I unlock the door and nudge it open. The hinges creak as the dark wood makes way to reveal a cozy bedroom. Like the rail car, two bunk beds are positioned on either side of the room. A desk sits against the wall between them, where I set Reo's duffel bags. James sets the snack satchel that Reo emptied down as well. The open window above the desk lets cool autumn air into the room. Tattered curtains with old, floral patterns wave in the breeze.

"Check out these blankets." I laugh, observing the dated bedding. Folded wool blankets with wintry moose patterns lay on the bed. James raises his eyebrows and smiles before flopping Soterios onto the bed. Wincing, he rubs the shoulder he carried Soterios with and moves that arm in a circular motion. His bones and joints crack and pop. I unfold Soterios' glasses and place them on his face.

His face looks almost lifeless.

Pale. Cold. Still.

No wonder people mistake vampires for the undead. I don't believe in resurrecting corpses, nor do I wish to. Though, I did witness Soterios come face to face with the grim reaper himself. I take a seat on the bed across from him and stare down at the maroon rug. My hands shake. I place my palms on my knees to ground myself. Tipping my head back, I take a deep breath. A lump swells in my throat.

"He isn't my friend," I assure myself. "He's boring and annoying and...and..."

James frowns. "It's okay to care. You can only run from your companionship for so long. He's a childhood friend, no? I thought I hated my father for disappearing again and again, but when he left for good, he took a piece of me with him. You feel that same piece slipping right now." James turns his back to me and shuts the door behind him on his way out of the room.

I deny everything.

After a hard swallow, I sit with my head in my hands. My nails dig into the thin skin of my forehead. How could I have become so attached? I should have helped him.

"But why?" I utter, gritting my teeth.

"Because he's weak," a deep voice answers me. I gasp, whipping my head around. It's the innkeeper. I curl my lips in, and the urge to defend Soterios grows within me.

"I—I—! He's not weak!"

"If he was strong, this wouldn't have happened."

"Why are you here, anyway!?" I snap, gnashing my teeth.

"Your companion told me to check on you. It's my job to tend to my guests," he clarifies. "Once upon a time, I was feeble. It's quite obvious. That's how I got myself roped into running this inn."

"Huh?"

He rolls up his sleeve to reveal an intricate brand that covers his arm like a tattoo. I assume it was physical proof of a contract.

"A foolish creature tricked me into this job. Now I'm bound to spend the rest of my life serving travelers," he informs me, pulling up a chair from the room's desk. "Like him," he raises his brows at Soterios, "I was too inexperienced."

"A creature? Not even a person?"

"Fiction is fact in this freaky world." He just laughs.

"Weirder things have happened," Soterios' voice interrupts us. My eyes quickly widen. I have never been so happy to hear his dull drone. Well, not *happy*. Relieved at most! "You're the man who stepped into the wrong fairy circle, right? That's what got you into the inn's contract." His gaze falls on the innkeeper's branded arm. "My mother used you as an example of what happens when one messes with faeries."

"You may put up a crappy fight, but hey, you're a bright kid."

Soterios awkwardly smiles. His happy expressions tend to lean on the stiff side even when he is sincere. He lifts his glasses off of his face, raising a single brow.

"You've never put glasses on before, have you?" He glances at me, almost amused as he flips his spectacles around and puts them back on his face.

Out of embarrassment, I don't make eye contact.

"I'm happy to see you're still clinging to life," I admit.

"Sometimes I question if it's worth it." Soterios rolls over to face the wall.

"Remember what you told me?" I lean down.

"I've told you many things."

I bite my lip.

"About that novel you were reading on the train. The one about secretive friendships and betrayal. Remember, you said that you wish to live a fulfilling life through the characters in it?"

"I'm surprised you can recall that," Soterios cuts me off before I can continue.

My cheeks grow warm in frustration. "You have friends, you know. And you can live a fulfilling life if you make an effort."

"Not like this."

"Yes, like this."

Silence falls over us.

"Soterios, look at me." I implore him with my eyes. His figure blurs as he slowly turns over to look at me. His eyes are swollen and his cheeks are pink. He rubs his red nose on his muddy sleeve. I forget about the innkeeper, who silently sits, watching us. Soterios' jaw quivers as it sits ajar, loosely hanging off of his bewildered face.

Soterios sighs, admitting, "You're right."

I smile as Soterios sits up. As my focus shifts back to my sight, I notice that my eyes sting from the glitched images that come into my vision, but I pay no mind to the pain.

"Promise me, from now on, you'll let me help you craft a life worth looking forward to."

I nod in response.

"Starting with this evening's meal. Your dinner should be ready by now," the innkeeper adds. Soterios smiles, but quickly seals his lips because the gruff host warns him, "Keep those teeth as concealed as much as possible, though."

"Yes, sir."

"Let's not have the bloody scare happen again." The innkeeper chuckles under his breath, not out of humor, but worry.

I raise a brow.

"Bloody scare?"

"It's a part of vampiric history. A few decades after Vylad had received his curse, the word about the bloodsucking, cursed species got out. Normal people were horrified. They kept crosses close by and wooden stakes on hand. Superstitious people still do the same."

Huh, so that's why my parents kept stakes by the front door when I was younger.

"Rumors got passed around like pamphlets. Before that time, Vylad and his people lived fairly normal lives, despite having fangs and bloodthirsty desires. Since the bloody scare, humans have despised vampires. People fear what they don't understand. They even made up nonsensical stories, such as vampires hating garlic and sunlight." The innkeeper leads us out of the room.

"The garlic idea came from the fact that two vampire twins despised the flavor. The sunlight sensitivity hoax came from Vyad's notoriously pale skin," Soterios helps him explain. I nod in comprehension. However, I do not wish for Vylad's image to come up in my mind again.

"He's as white as a ghost." The man laughs.

"You know him?" Soterios inquires.

"We were close acquaintances when I was a lad. We've grown apart since then. Are you familiar with him?"

"Yes. He saved my life." Soterios continues his eternal streak of being upfront with strangers and straight to the point. Some people never change.

"Oh really?" The innkeeper's intonation rises.

"I have no reason to lie about such things. That was our only encounter. Everything else I know about him is from textbooks. The writers were undoubtedly biased against Vylad, along with the rest of his cursed kind."

I can't imagine all of my knowledge coming from books. I don't have a bunch of 'real-life experiences,' but at least what I know isn't from boring textbooks. I'm the type to listen to my grandfathers at family gatherings. Each and every elder in my family has an epic full of tall tales to tell me. As the only grandchild, they pass their knowledge on to me, in hopes that I continue to recite their stories. Little do they know, I'm more interested in making my own.

We reach the bottom of the stairs and step into the parlor.

"What took you weirdos so long?" Reo scolds us from the dining area. James stays silent, as he is a fellow of few words.

"None of your business," I reply, heading over.

"Don't pull that one on me again! You say that just because you have something to hide!" he whines.

"Or do I?" I grin. Reo pounds his fists on his table, making the silverware slightly shake.

We feast on steak, mashed potatoes, and rolls. Our sweet bread is served with us with delectable homemade cinnamon butter. I fill up my plate for the third time and glance over my shoulder to find that Soterios is still picking at his first. His lips stay sealed for the entire meal.

"It's good, isn't it?" I ask.

He nod. His slim fingers ever so slightly tremble as he holds his fork in one hand and his knife in the other.

"Still thinking about Vylad?" Reo nags him.

James nudges him, leans over, and grumbles something into Reo's ear. He quickly sucks his lips in.

"Yes."

I have to admit, I had been thinking about Vylad, too. *What hidden motive did he have? Ulterior plan?* Tapping my foot on the ground helps ease my stress over Soterios' current condition. Vylad's return is my biggest concern, other than Soterios' current situation.

"It's frustrating, people's fear of what they fail to fathom. It's not fair. Vampires didn't do anything. Just because someone is different doesn't mean that..." Soterios trails off. He sets his utensils down. He raises his voice more than usual. "I don't want to end up shunned like *them*."

The sudden outburst causes others to take notice. A muscular adult makes his way over to the table. His fingertips curling around the handle of his steak knife, Soterios glances up at him. The man grabs onto the collar of Soterios' bloodied sweater and yanks him out of his chair. Mustering up the strength, Soterios pulls away, but the man grabs his forearm and tugs him into the center of the dining area. In surprise, Soterios gasps and his pearly fangs glisten under the candle-lit chandelier. I cringe.

"I knew it," the man snarls.

Quickly turning the tables, Soterios presses the knife's serrated blade against the man's neck. His face, as always, displays no emotion. On the contrary, his attacker, who is now the attacked, has a red face and sweat rolling down his forehead. His jaw remains clamped shut. The only sounds to be heard are the man's deep breaths and another's mysterious clapping. I turn to see the innkeeper behind us.

"If you're going to pick fights," he announces, "at least do it with someone your own size. He's just a lad, Greg."

His nose scrunches. "He doesn't belong here. *They* don't belong here." He gestures to Soterios, adding, "He has a knife to my throat, Derek."

Soterios lowers the sharp utensil before straightening his glasses.

"Well, well, well. Look who's feeling better." Reo smirks, swaying from side to side in his seat.

"A bit, thanks to this innkeeper's hospitality. I could be much worse," Soterios responds and gestures toward Derek. He sits back down in his chair, his hands folded in his lap, his fingers uncomfortably curled.

Greg shoots Derek a dirty glare before sneering, "I thought you knew better than to shelter a filthy bloodsucker." He merely smiles and offers him a drink on the house to calm his temper, which Greg hesitantly accepts.

"Sometimes fate deals men a hand of cards that does not work in their favor. It is those who gawk at their uncontrolled misfortune who make that hand despicable," Derek tells Greg as he guides him by the shoulders to the bar area. "This boy just happened to get the short end of the stick."

James had finished his dinner before we came downstairs, so he patiently waits for the rest of us. Reo has to be on his fourth or fifth helping. I can't help but think he looks like a plump chipmunk with too much food stuffed in its tiny mouth. Unlike him, I am too full to help myself to another serving after my first plate. Soterios seems to feel the same way. I'm surprised to find that only small crumbs and brown smears of gravy remain on his plate as he stands up.

"I don't think I'll ever be able to eat again." At last, Reo flails his arms and belches.

"Excuse you." James frowns at his poor behavior.

"*Nuh-uh*, excuse you," Reo sneers back at him. He glances at me, asking in a hushed voice, "Is Soterios going to be okay?"

I shrug. "I have no idea. You'll need to ask him."

"His response before was too vague. I don't think he likes me." Reo rolls his eyes.

"Imagine that. Even I can't stand you at times," James quietly mocks Reo as he looks away. His face flushes a bright shade of crimson and pulls his woven scarf up to his nose to cover his lips and blushing cheeks. The events of the day have obviously gotten our emotions as disheveled and messy as we look.

Derek's inn turns out to be the perfect place for us to have stopped. The innkeeper not only provides us with a room to stay in but also a change of clothes. After promptly cleaning ourselves up, we put the day to rest.

I wake up to the faint chords of a piano. It is a beautiful piece. One that I have never heard before. I squint to find the curtains fluttering in the midnight breeze. A huge blue moon peeks out from behind the clouds in an otherwise starless sky. The celestial mass' brightness overwhelms me. The strange music in conjunction with the eerie moonlight soothes me, yet, at the same time, disturbs me. I put all of my focus into seeing only in the moment as I slip out of bed. I use a flame spell to light a half-melted candle to guide me through the darkness. A creaking noise escapes the hinges as I open the door, and I check to see if everyone else is still asleep. There are no murmurs or movements. I make my way down the stairs as quietly as possible in search of the musician. The further I descend the stairs, the stronger the music grows. The pianist has properly brought the somber sentiment woven into the piece to life.

Entering the parlor, I look around in search of the piano. It waits in the corner. I recall that a woman had been knitting there earlier. A single player now sits before it with a jar of fireflies on their right illuminating the ivory keys. They do not notice my presence. I'm tempted to greet them, but feel bad disturbing the song, so I sit down on the couch and listen. The heavy keys contain hints of lingering sorrows. Orange light from the town's oil lamp posts seeps into the room through the parlor's grand front windows. The warm rays do not reach the pianist. Instead, they cast a shadow over them, concealing their identity. The pianist hits and draws out the last key before the world feels like it is entirely still.

My claps fracture the silence. The pianist flinches. I stand up and walk into the tavern area, but do not reach the piano. I hesitate.

"Julius?" the shadowy figure asks. "I was not aware that another would be up at this hour."

"I was not aware that you played the piano." My eyes widen. I can not begin to imagine how a boy with such flat-affect could play an instrument that evokes such complex emotions. I don't have to imagine him. He's right here in front of me.

"I started playing when I was five. You really didn't know?"

"To be honest, it's not like I paid any mind to you before."

"I know."

"B—but you know that changed, right?"

"I know."

"Well, uh, you play really well."

Soterios is taken aback by my compliment. "Thanks."

"If you don't mind me asking, why did you come down here in the first place?"

Soterios falls silent as he pulls down the wooden piano cover. His eyes avoid contact with mine as his mouth opens, trying to find words to say.

"You know. Because of the vampiric transformation, being around others is difficult."

"Because of the blood thing?"

"Yes. It is the last stage of the conversion."

"Can't you stop it by not, y'know, sucking blood?"

"No. It's not that simple. I'll go mad."

"Can't we turn back time?"

"In less than three days, of course not. Even if we did manage to create a time machine, time only progresses forwards. There's no undo button. Once the curse takes effect on the body, the victim has to accept their fate or die trying to resist."

I bite my lip, ironically, before considering what I am offering, "You can take mine?"

"What?"

"Yeah, uh." I pull down the side of my shirt so that my neck is exposed. "Vampires usually bite here, right?"

Soterios creases his eyebrows. "How do you know that?"

"People have been writing about vampires for centuries. I'm pretty familiar with the lore."

In all honesty, the vampire films and literature I had consumed as a kid still haunt me to this day. Most of it was contraband fiction from the Overworld, even though its inhabitants don't truly understand vampires. Even some people in the Mirror Realm fail to grasp the concept of and story behind the cursed race. Out of all the films I've watched, most of it is romance. *Cliché*, I know.

Soterios sighs. "The neck contains one's carotid artery, which carries blood from the heart to the brain."

A lump grows in the back of my throat. "Will I get brain damage?"

"No, I don't believe so."

"Ok and I definitely won't become a vampire, right?"

"No, the transformation *only* happens when a human consumes a vampire's blood."

The image of Vylad cutting his own thumb with his sharp, black nails flashes in my brain. I take a deep breath in. "Okay, then I'm ready when you're ready."

"Don't tense up," Soterios advises me as he stands up. I turn my face away as he bows his head. I want to cry out for help the moment his fangs pierce the skin of my neck. It was like not one, but two needles jabbing into my body and draining what I think is massive amounts of blood. I have never felt that before, but that's what I assumed it was like. My whole body freezes. Soterios pulls away, gasping for breath. He bumps into the piano behind him and sinks down, pressing his knees against his chest.

"I'm sorry. I'm so sorry." He keeps apologizing over and over again, rubbing the blood from his cheeks onto his sleeves.

I cut him off. "Stop, Soterios. It's okay."

I've never ever seen him this close to crying. In fact, before I was convinced that he was not capable of shedding tears.

"It's not. It's really not. Nothing can justify my actions. Nothing can justify my helplessness. I should have just died."

"Don't say that. You took a stab to the stomach for me. You saved my life. I—I couldn't save yours when you needed me, so this is the least I can do."

Soterios pulls his glasses off. Slow tears roll down his smooth, freckled face, glistening in the soft light. I kneel before him with my hands out slightly, unsure of what to do. Nobody has ever cried in front of me before. His weeping breaks my heart. The bridge of my nose stings as my lips uncontrollably tremble.

"I really do wish there was an undo option in life. With all my existence, I long for such a conquest," Soterios pulls himself together. "But it's better to be a realist than delusional."

"Hey, that wizard we're supposed to be finding, maybe he can help you too!" Even with my uneasy voice, I try to make him feel better or at least give him some sort of hope.

"Right." He stands and puts his glasses back on.

I awake to the sound of singing birds. Soterios is sitting in the windowsill, his knees pulled to his chest. His once gray eyes, now scarlet from the curse, watch the chirping birds. A serene sense of tranquility fills the room. I keep silent. He hasn't noticed me yet.

"Oh, you're up." Soterios turns to me.

After yawning, I nod. "Yep, bright and early."

"Right." He glances at the rising sun. "It should be about six-thirty."

"You can tell time just by looking at the sun?" I squint, shielding my eyes from the light. *Ugh*, it's too early for his nerdy nonsense. Though, telling time with the sun in the Mirror Realm is not too difficult. After all, celestial masses rise and set like clockwork. Streaks of vibrant hues of red, orange, and yellow fill the sky. The silhouettes of rooftops craft the horizon. An enormous castle looms in the distance, at the center of the capital. The light blue glow of daytime slowly casts down upon the city from above.

"I learned how to read the sun when I was younger. It was required for school." He slides down from the windowsill and straightens his glasses. The sickly past version of him has been left behind. Yesterday's blood has revived him. "One could say it's second nature by now."

"Oh, uh, what about Reo and James?" I realize they're not in the room. "Where are they?"

"Downstairs eating breakfast."

"Why haven't you joined them?"

"I was waiting for you."

I rub the side of my neck. The tips of my fingers brush two tiny scabs. A small bruise festers around them. When I move my neck, I can feel a slight throb. I remind myself that this mild suffering is only to make up for him saving my life not once, but twice.

"Thanks."

He nods.

Sure enough, Reo and James are waiting for us at last night's dinner table. Reo has already started his daily slandering of unfortunate civilians. On the other hand, James quietly waits for us with his hands folded in his lap.

"My bad. I would've gotten up earlier if I knew you guys would have to wait."

Honestly, I don't mean that. Six-thirty is far too early for me. I have a tendency to sleep in until noon, or even past then. On the other hand, I make a habit of staying up until midnight. Dark circles under my eyes today will not be a surprise. This morning, they feel unusually tired and strange.

James' eyes widen before he laughs. "You're like a rock, so we didn't bother trying."

I awkwardly chuckle under my breath in response and have a seat next to James. Before Soterios sits down, he quickly scans the room. For what? I am not sure.

Maybe the man from yesterday's supper? Though, I think they have already come to terms thanks to Derek. Maybe he is searching for the innkeeper to thank him, but I don't think Soterios is that type of person. He's grateful for many things, yet isn't vocal about expressing his gratitude.

As if conjured up by my thoughts, the innkeeper delivers empty breakfast plates to each of us. He places a tower of blueberry pancakes in the center of our circular table. The rumbling of my stomach longs for food. Reo licks his lips.

"Hitting the road so soon?" he asks gruffly.

"Yep, we've got places to go!" Reo grins, forking three pancakes at once onto his plate.

"Will you be enjoying the royal family's festivities? People travel from far and wide to come here. You probably saw the decorations as you came in."

"We'll see." Reo shrugs. From his forcibly calm tone, his excitement is disguised, but I still know that his answer is a definite yes.

Reo, of course, drags us through the city streets. He pulls me and Soterios by our wrists. I'd be able to better enjoy this event if Reo isn't in control. As always, his annoying habits distract from the live folk music, the aroma of street food, and the overall splendid day. I pull away from his grasp and begin to explore on my

own. Soterios tags along while the two others go on their way. The sun's rays warm my skin, and a gentle breeze blows by to take summer's lingering heat away. Autumn leaves jumble around, making their way to the ground.

Unexpectedly, another vision fills my mind, similar to the one I experienced on the Sunset Train.

This time, the horned boy takes a girl with hair the shade of campfire flames by the hand as they run through bustling city streets, much like these. His sudden enthusiasm catches her off guard, but her surprised expression mellows into a subtle smile. The two explore the crowded village. Even amongst nobles, sorceresses, and elves, they can't help but stand out. The boy tucks a lock of the girl's slick orange hair behind her ear, fastening it into place with a flowery hairpin. Though their mouths open to speak, I can not make out their conversation. Young and old couples gather together in the center of town. The girl takes the boy by his forearm and guides him into the center of the action. Despite his efforts to pull away, he gives in and holds the girl's hands. Her smile brightens as the two spin and weave through the other duets.

My reverie ends as I snap back to my reality, to the current festival.

I grumble for a moment, the duo still on my mind. If only I wasn't ditched by Lauralyn in the forest.

A curly-haired girl, her short locks the color of snow catches my eye. As I squint to focus, I notice that her eyes are the shade of wild hyacinths. Antlers protrude from either side of her head. To my surprise, she makes her way over to us. I grin, wondering if this is my chance to

replace that heinous black-haired traitor. She stops in front of Soterios and places her hand on his cheek. His red eyes jerk open.

"Fascinating. A vampire amidst a crowd of humans." A jubilant smile appears on her face as she glances over at me. "And...you're friends?"

After a moment of hesitation, I nod. Soterios does the same.

"I knew it!" She throws her arms around Soterios, who stumbles backward. "See, I told Avi everyone can be friends." She takes a step back, but still clings to Soterios' hands. "You know, I used to be close friends with a vampire. Since our parting, I haven't seen another."

He stares at her for a moment. I can sense that he wants to tell her that he wasn't always a vampire.

"Here we are." He raises his hands.

"Though, that's odd. Usually, vampires have perfect vision, but you have glasses."

Soterios falls silent.

"Don't you know that you don't need them? Those red eyes of yours have twenty-twenty vision, if you haven't noticed already. But if you've been living with glasses all your life, then it wouldn't hurt to keep them. I think they're pretty cool. Do replace the prescription with normal glass. It'll harm your perception of the world if you keep them like this."

I cross my arms and anxiously tap my foot on the brick road. *I'm not jealous*, I assure myself, even though Soterios is getting all of the attention.

"Oh, thank you." His fangs reveal themselves as he tries his best to smile at the girl.

My hands shift to rest on my hips. "You look...free-spirited, and," I gesture to her antlers, "forest-y. We're looking for a wizard named Zacharias. Do you know who he is and where we can find him?"

"Yes. Well, sort of." She turns to look at me. As my vision comes into focus, I can't tell if the lavender-colored markings on her face are natural or painted on. "An acquaintance of mine knows both him and his whereabouts."

"Can you arrange a meeting?" I raise a brow.

The girl's expression droops as her gaze shifts off to the side. "I doubt he'll let me ask a favor of him. After all, I wasn't supposed to come here."

"Oh, right. This kingdom isn't very welcoming, to say the least." I uncomfortably rub the back of my neck.

"Despite over half of its territory's population being fairies and elven folk," she adds to my sentence with a sigh. "Last week alone, five elves were imprisoned for '*trespassing*.'"

"I heard it's better than in the past. The knights were commanded to 'kill-on-sight' as recently as a few years ago," Soterios expounds on the matter.

The girl nods. "Though, unfortunately, that is still the case for vampires. So please be cautious."

I grimace for a moment, wondering what would happen to Soterios if he was discovered by the knights. He already caused a ruckus last night at dinner. Luckily, the innkeeper was there to protect him. Strong people like him will not always be around. Maybe it's best to stay out of major towns and villages, especially in the kingdom of Milledale.

"I'm Astoria, by the way. Please excuse my delayed introduction." She slightly bows to us. Her antlers almost whack Soterios in the chin.

"The name's Julius." I point to myself using my thumb, keeping the rest of my fingers balled up in a fist.

Soterios simply states his given name and surname. Soterios Solace.

Honestly, I envy his name. It gives an air of importance and commands attention. Mine is so boring. I've heard of many Juliuses in history, but he is the only Soterios I know. Plus, Solace sounds so much cooler than Subedar. The alliteration of Soterios Solace rolls off the tongue. Julius Subedar doesn't have that flair.

I expect to hear two more names, but Reo and James' introductions do not follow. I remember that they wandered off on their own to enjoy the royal festivities. They're nearly inseparable, like a parent and child. The younger of the two, James, being the adult and the elder, Reo, being the child. They really are a dysfunctional duo.

People in costumes, floral accessories, and headdresses frolick down the street, dodging our trio in their paths. Some frown at us while others compliment Astoria's enchanting appearance. She is definitely prettier than Lauralyn, who could have been compared to a corpse. I like the way her smile gently eases into her round cheeks and swirly purple markings. The faces of our two missing friends are still nowhere to be seen. That's probably for the better.

Nevermind.

As pounding footsteps approach, a boastful voice exclaims from behind, "We found someone who knows Zacharias!"

Chapter 5:
The Guide

"Astoria, I don't know what to say about this." Avi, the boy James and Reo brought to us, lectured her for the next few minutes about venturing into town without permission. He had pulled us away from all of the "nonsense," "danger," and "chaos" of the festival, and into the woods. To me, the forest is far, *far* more perilous than the town. Obviously, as an elven creature, she is at a high risk and, apparently, she isn't too well-versed with the geography or social constructs of the kingdom. Like a father scolding his young daughter, compassion silently stood behind his stern words and bold warnings. Soterios and I listened without saying a word. As his lecture progressed, we realized we had followed him deeper and deeper into the forest.

Halfway through, James and Reo turned back. Reo insisted that he couldn't listen to Avi anymore, and James planned on returning to the inn, in hopes of connecting with his father. From

there, I assume they'll take the train back to Medenelle. James will fill in for his mother, once again while Reo will return to his successful life in the Overworld, where he has both status and power he wasn't able to find in our realm. I find it difficult to imagine how much of an ego-crusher his anonymity in the Mirror Realm must be for him. I'm glad to get Reo off of our backs, but still grateful for his monetary resources, along with James' medical assistance and favorable connections. I understand, however, this is not their journey to partake in. Soterios and I can take it from here.

"Enough of that. What brings these two to your attention?" Avi, our new guide, runs his fingers along his tall, jackal-like ears. He flicks a bell earring that softly jiggles before crossing his arms.

"Didn't you hear what the others remarked? They're looking for Zacharias!"

Avi's already displeased expression droops further as he stares up at Astoria, who is about a head taller than him. He looks no older than fourteen, nor is he taller than youth around that age. From his maturity and dialect, I can tell that he is much older than he appears to be. Many humanoid creatures, like elves and vampires, tend to display age very differently than mankind.

"You're pulling my tails."

A bouquet of fluffy tails sway behind his back. Both his curly hair and dark brown fur have a slight green tint. There's no end to the surprises I have encountered in the forest. I can't help but worry about the wizard.

Astoria shakes her head. Avi sighs and pulls his black cloak tighter. Stacked golden circlets that cover his neck and shoulders peek out from under the cloth. Crystals and engravings adorn his extravagant jewelry. "Very well then."

He leads our group into a clearing. Humble huts made of leaves and wood pepper the perimeter. In these homes, woodland folk rest on porches, cook meals, knit, or even meditate with burning incense. Many have facial markings, like Avi and Astoria, and vibrant hair colors of all shades, spanning from deep blue to flaming red. Their proximity to Milledale's capital is risky. It's a wonder they haven't been discovered. Zacharias can't be too far away.

We're so close! I assure myself. *I'll understand this curse and Soterios could become human again!*

As I let the thought sink in, Avi tells us that he needs to grab a few supplies and trots off, into one of the houses.

Astoria giggles. "What's that giddy smirk on your face for?"

"Huh? Nothing!" My cheeks grow warm as I turn away. Even Soterios is mildly amused by my defensive reply. From his somewhat uneasy expression, I can tell that he knows something that I don't. The thought concerns me.

Avi's earring jingles once more as he returns, capturing my attention. Soterios turns to our guide as well. Like in cartoons, a colorful bag hangs from a shepherd's crook that Avi carries over his shoulder.

"We don't have all day, lazies. When we arrive at the purple trail intersection, you'll get another break and we'll stop for lunch. The sun should be at high noon by then." Our leader nearly leaves us in the dust.

Maybe pancakes aren't enough for breakfast, I wonder as doubt grows within me. My stomach, on the verge of growling, rebels against our plans. Avi takes us through the woods, yet again, but at least we're now on a walking path. We no longer need to dodge trees and shake loose leaves off of our shoes. Layered roots form natural stairs. Astoria, who decided to tag along, tries sparking up conversations.

"Why are you looking for Zacharias?"

I try explaining to her how I got cursed, but the story ends up making Soterios and me seem foolish. Astoria giggles at us. I turn

my head away. Soterios does the same. Avi is almost amused by our misfortune, yet somehow his delight fails to surprise me. He feels like the type of person to merely let out a soft chuckle before commenting, "*Hmph*, kids these days."

Without a second of hesitation, that is his exact reply to our tall tale.

"There's nothing wrong with a misadventure," Astoria tries to stand up for us with her cheeks puffed out. "I've had many myself."

Avi sighs with the shake of his head.

"For the longest time I was missing an antler. I tumbled down a staircase and just snapped off," Astoria admits out of the blue. I scan her antlers. Little flowers sprout around the branches. They show no sign of her confessed clumsiness.

"Tripping over one's feet and getting cursed are very different afflictions," Avi immediately invalidates her self-proclaimed misadventure. "I've noticed a strange uptick in curses and charms lately. They've never been this common."

I expect him to go on rambling about the subject, and so he does. He explains how rare it is to see two cursed or charmed people in one room and how the chances of them knowing each other are even less.

"I always wanted to be charmed," he murmurs, looking up to the sky. Rays of light from the blue abyss rain down on us from between the thick leaves. This forest's aura puts the one back home to shame. Life blossoms all around us. "Zacharias once told me that they connect you to the innermost depths of our world. I'm quite jealous of you two, but honestly, I'm rather thankful that I am not a vampire. It's not like I don't live in hiding already. Having a charm myself would allow me to deepen my studies—"

"You came out today," Astoria interjects, cutting Avi off mid-sentence.

"That was an emergency." His cheeks flush red before he carries on with the hike.

Astoria subconsciously curls her fingers around the fabric of her dress and tugs on the sides as she trots down the path. I find her hiking boots to be cute, yet not very fitting for her outfit. I usually assume that a down-to-earth girl who lives in the woods would wear less fancy clothing made for function, rather than fashion. Reo would be in full support of her wardrobe choices. The silky fabric of her dress is embroidered with golden swirls and lace playfully peeks out from beneath the hem. Little tears and splatters of mud tatter her lower half.

I notice Astoria sneaking glances in Soterios' direction. She seems particularly enthralled by his red irises. On occasion, I catch myself staring as well. Scarlet, shimmering eyes stand out as much as sore, throbbing thumbs. Especially when I'm accustomed to looking into his dull, gray eyes.

I tear my gaze away from Soterios and find myself analyzing Avi's skin tone, sun-kissed and speckled with traces of many years spent with nature. His face is much darker than mine, and as a stark contrast of Astoria's, whose skin is almost the shade of her wintry hair. Even darker freckles dot his cheeks. I wonder how extensive his travels have been. He's clearly not native to this area. Sunlight filtering through the branches enhances highlights in his hair that I did not see before. The jewelry Avi conceals with his cloak jingles as he walks, along with the tiny bell clipped to his ear.

Though silence falls upon our group, the symphony of nature around us fills the empty space. Beyond the trees, I pick up the rushing of a small brook's stream tumbling over eroding stones in its ever-flowing path. Leaves crunch under our feet, but also rustle above. Forest critters chatter and scurry about. My gaze lingers somewhere in the abyss of golden trees. The vision impairments I've been facing cease to infiltrate my perception of the world in

these moments. I see why people like Avi and Astoria choose to live a life in the forest, one with nature, nearly free from the shackles of society and ever-evolving lifestyles.

Up ahead, I catch sight of a trailhead and another path that comes in contact with ours. I grin. I'm tempted to do a little celebratory dance. Lunch!

Avi suddenly stops before we reach the crossing, so Astoria does the same. Soterios and I follow. In search of a reason, I glance at Avi, who is staring up at the sky. His ear twitches, ringing the jingle bell.

"Did you hear that?"

The three of us exchange confused glances before shaking our heads. Avi crosses his arms with a small harumph.

"The rustling leaves. Someone is following us."

"It must be a squirrel. There's no one else around." Astoria's eyebrows draw together, and her eyes dart around, scanning the surrounding forest. Everything remains still. I keep my eyes on the crossing up ahead. My stomach urges me to continue on. I subconsciously gnaw on the inside of my cheek to distract from my hunger and ease the anticipation. A large gust of wind howls through the trees. No footsteps follow.

"False alarm?" I impatiently tilt my head.

Avi begrudgingly admits that I'm right and allows us to move forward.

I reach the crossing first and lean against the side of the wooden trail marker pole, which slightly shifts under my weight. Two painted arrows point in corresponding directions with their trail, ours being the yellow path, the other being the purple path. Avi takes a seat on a fallen log and opens up his bag, revealing our lunch. Astoria and Soterios sit on either side of him. Their feet touch the ground, but Avi's don't come close to touching the forest floor.

He portions out our meal: two perfect sandwiches. The cream-colored bread has no dents or imperfections, no holes or air bubbles like the discounted goods my family purchases from the local bakery. Little ruffles of lettuce peek out from the sides, along with tomatoes and slivers of meat. Each sandwich has been split into equal triangular halves. He hands a slice to me first. Then one to Astoria, and finally Soterios.

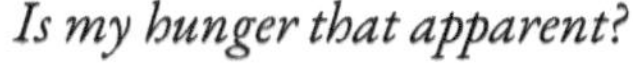

Is my hunger that apparent?

I smile, yet my cheek still twitches out of embarrassment. The sandwich tastes just as good as it looks. I only wish that there was more. Of course, that's greedy, but half of a sandwich is by all means not a suitable lunch. Soterios' poor appetite leads him to offer me the remainder of his sandwich that I gladly accept without hesitation. I practically inhale his gracious grant. Avi scoffs at me as he slides off of the log and onto his feet. His cloak flutters, but still doesn't give me a good look at his outfit underneath. I find it difficult not to see him as a huge shawl with a head and tiny feet.

"Was that enough of a break for you?" Avi implores.

I want to reply no, but end up nodding instead. Finding Zacharias is the top priority right now for both Soterios' sake and my own.

"Astoria, I trust that you know the path back to camp." Avi turns to her. "The rest of the quest is for us. One day you'll get the chance to meet Zacharias, but not today."

"Aw, okay." She sighs. "I'll find my way back."

Before leaving, Astoria gives both of us a warm hug, me under one arm and Soterios under the other. It's a bittersweet goodbye,

but I assume that our paths will cross again. Avi refuses to give out hugs.

We continue our journey down the yellow path. Even though he's not the jolliest soul, Avi whistles as we hike down the path. With every step we take, the trail gets more and more overgrown. Though Avi doesn't seem bothered, Soterios pulls thorns out of his sleeves. I push branches out of my face and kick brambles aside. I wonder who last traversed this route.

"Are we there yet?" I groan, dragging my toes with each and every step I take.

"Are you going to stop asking that?"

"Well, yeah. When we get there."

Avi rolls his eyes, including his head in the circular motion. He has the fullest of rights to do so. I bet Soterios has been silently keeping track of how many times I've pestered Avi. He used to count every time I asked that question when we were kids, whether we were on horseback, on a hike, or driving in the Overworld. I can't imagine loving numbers so much.

Yuck. Count me out.

To my suprise, we arrive at the mouth of a cave.

"Zacharias!" Avi calls out, but his voice weakly projects into the cave.

I shout the stranger's name as well, followed by a, "You there?"

A dark figure emerges. He pushes the flowering vines out of his way with two arms, but another pair stays by his side. I gulp. What sort of creature has four arms? When we spoke of wizards before, I imagined an old man with a long, white beard and a blue constellation-patterned gown. Before me stands a lanky, multi-limbed man, looking to be in his mid-twenties. His light eyes lock their sights on us while a toothy white grin spreads across his mulberry face. For some reason, his smile intimidates me far more than Vylad's fangs. I wince.

"My, my. What do we have here? Ah, my beloved, Avi!"

Avi salutes. The bell earring of his jingles. Zacharias snickers at the adorable sound, teasing Avi about how cute he is. Our surly, short-statured guide provides no response to Zacharias' provoking, though his bronze cheeks redden.

"These travelers are in search of your help." He gestures toward me and Soterios. Like Avi, I stiffly salute him. Soterios just nods.

"We need your help to control my curse and rid Soterios of his."

Zacharias' smile fades into mild despair.

"Oh, I can't assist you with that."

Despite denying us assistance, he invites us into the cave. Zacharias tells Avi that if he's not here to 'crack the books,' then he should 'buzz off,' which he does without hesitation. With a frown, Zacharias waves our guide off. He murmurs about Avi being such a great spellcaster, but so unwilling to refine his craft and turn his natural talent into polished skill.

"Anywho," Zacharias teasingly addresses us, "you know removing a curse is basically impossible, right?" He picks up a half-melted candle with one hand and ignites it with the fingertips of another hand. He wears a black turtleneck that almost blends into the shadows, cargo pants, and weathered hiking boots. The frayed laces dangle by the soles of his shoes, almost tripping him every other step. The further he leads us into his lair, the more luminous the crystals grow on the walls. Water rich with minerals runs off of stalactites.

"Yes," Soterios responds.

"Eastern cultures have found ways to draw out curses, but that requires a living sacrifice, which I refuse to take such extreme measures. My status among humans is awful already."

I swallow hard. "I heard you're eccentric, but your knowledge about curses and charms is what brought us here, along with your magic skills."

"Magic skills? I *am* magic, dear." His giggles teeter on the line of comedy and insanity.

Yep, he's crazy, I silently confirm to myself.

"The majority of the spells you use today are works of my hands and fruits of my many, many, many studies." He stops and spins around on one heel. Tiny, colorful sparks circle in the air illuminating the cavern walls, along with the white freckles on Zacharias' cheeks.

Finishing his flourish, Zacharias stops to get a good look at us. "Look, homeboy, you're a vampire now. Obviously you're new to this gig. You don't need these anymore." He plucks Soterios' glasses off of his nose. He pauses for a moment with the glasses tightly gripped in his hands. I stare at his pointed nails and quivering fingertips. His eyes gloss over for a tiny moment, as if transported to the past only to remember that those moments will forever stay as faded memories.

Soterios without glasses is a strange sight to behold. His face feels empty. His fingers twitch, itching to get his spectacles back. Zaharias uses one set of thumbs to push out the lenses. The glass circles pop out of the frames and fall to the cave's cold, stone floor. They land at two different times with soft *plinks* that echo throughout the musty cavern. Without warning, Soterios' lensless glasses are shoved back onto his face. Despite the aggressive gesture, Soterios seems relieved to have his spectacles back, as if his identity is intertwined with the thin-wired frame.

"So...is there anything you can do to help us?" Tapping my foot on the ground, I grow impatient. We came this far. There's no way I'm giving up and turning back. After all, I swore to fix this before facing my mother and father. As if running away wasn't enough, my selfish deeds put Soterios in danger. Now we're both cursed, and there's no reverse. Zacharias glances over at me, smirking. I get a feeling that this won't be the last ominous grin he'll toss my way.

And this isn't the first, either.

"You've been having visions that you don't understand, right? When you were being examined by that medic, you saw the future, did you not? We just need to train your little pea brain to accept and comprehend this charm's power."

"Hey! Don't call me a peabrain!" I shout before his statement settles in. I might be shallow, but stupid is one thing I am not. "Wait, how do you know that?" My eyebrows draw together.

"Oh, I've been watching you the entire time."

Chapter 6:

The Tenet

W*ell, isn't that nice to know?* I flinch as my eye twitches. Those feelings of being watched. That prickly prey presence. The footsteps Avi stopped for. It was him all along.

"And Avi. And Astoria. I look after everyone who enters the forests of the Mirror Realm."

Zacharias opens a wooden fairy door hinged into the cave's wall. He can't possibly fit, after all, he towers over the two of us, probably standing no less than six feet tall. Despite his height, he bends down and effortlessly enters the tiny passageway. I follow, less gracefully, hitting my forehead on the cave's rock wall above the doorway on my way through.

He snarkily remarks, "Ya should've seen that coming," with an amused eye roll. He's already making puns about my curse? Right after he insulted my intellect? How low can this magic man go? Low enough to creep through the freakish fairy door.

"In order to traverse every forest, you must utilize teleportation magic, right?" Soterios questions Zacharias. "There's no other way to cover so many acres."

Zacharias nods with a grin. "*Hmph*, if only everyone had that intuition. I learned it from a friend. I'm sure you know my name by now, but I have not properly introduced myself. I am Zacharias, purveyor of wisdom and seeker of truth in this wretched world. In short, I study curses, like Avi. After all, I was the first one to be

cursed by *It*. And this," he continues and waves us in with his arms, "is my humble little dwelling."

As he rambles on, he plops down in an old armchair. The fairy entrance was quite misleading. There's plenty of room for creatures of any height. On the far wall of his home, there are shelves upon shelves of books, potions, bottled ingredients, and artifacts. A mug of wands sits on a desk among a sea of papers full of notes and diagrams. Chairs and furniture are strewn about, so I sit on a little stool with a quilted cushion on top. Candles and jars full of fireflies light the cavern. This place is cozy enough, but I wonder if Zacharias feels isolated here in the middle of nowhere.

I raise my brows. "You're cursed?"

"Cursed, charmed. Potato, potato. Tomato, tomato. I'd rather not dwell on the topic. Anyway, to me, you look like you have your curse under control. The threads of fate tugged on your vision before, but you're beyond that now."

"Then what do I need to do?" I bite my lip and lean forward.

"So quick to do, yet so slow to comprehend. That's the problem with youth. Before you look into the future, you must understand what sets it up, who paves that path."

"Don't we control what happens?"

"No, Stupid. Fate does." Zacharias leans back in his armchair. He laces his lanky fingers together. "Every little action has been planned in advance. What you say next has already been determined. Each blink and exhale have all been premeditated by a being I like to call *Fate*. This curse of yours connects your mind to

the pages of these plans. You can catch glimpses of what will come in the next chapters of life."

He proceeds to pester me in order to find out what bits of the future I had seen in my visions. I tell him about the horned soldier I saw on the train, and the vision of him and the redheaded girl I witnessed at the festival. His eyes sparkle at the mention of the two youths. To be honest, I still have no idea who they are, where they are, how old they are, or if they even exist yet. My vision of them only scratched the surface of the future of their lives and told me nothing about their past.

Zacharias abruptly stands and requests some time alone. He exits the cave, leaving Soterios and me by ourselves. I'm tempted to rummage through Zacharias' collection of rare items on his back wall, but I resist. I keep my hands to myself because I know better than to touch another's belongings. Who knows, someone might actually get poisoned again. Getting cursed is more than enough for me.

His departure gives me some time to think about what Zacharias told me. Finding out that fate exists conflicts with what I had been taught in church and by my parents for my whole life. Is Fate the equivalent of God? Or some entity that has yet to be contrived by mankind for them to worship? As for the life I've lived up until now, have I not been in control for a single moment? Is *Fate* a puppeteer pulling on his dolls' strings? I want to believe that Zacharias is wrong.

Zacharias returns from his venture with a handful of berries and three fish clenched in each of his other hands. I watch him mash the berries in a porcelain bowl. He puts the fish on skewers and roasts them over an open flame created by his palm. As he prepares our supper, I come to find that he's more reputable than I first gave him credit for. He tells us a little more about Fate. Apparently, the two aren't strangers. Zacharias had interacted with her on numerous occasions.

Female and accessible. Definitely not God, I think.

"As much as she fights for complete control, people still break free. She might write that someone falls down, but instead, they stumble." Zacharias adds, turning around to face us. "The moment our existence was manifested into being, there has been an opposing force. I think you two are rather familiar with that entity, no? It's *It*. Like a ripple, the defiance spreads from *It*'s actions, like when *It* cursed you in that cult-riddled forest."

My eyebrows draw together as I remember the shadowy creature.

"If what you said about *It* cursing you first holds true, then you're not bound to Fate's scriptures," Soterios conjectures.

Zacharias' eyes widen before his gaze softens. "You're not wrong. I should have died hundreds of years ago, but, alas, here I am cooking to feed an eternal body. Curses, as you know, manifest in many ways. Mine merely spared me from my frail mortal body, yet I'm condemned to live as an exile in this one."

I swallow hard and bite my lip.

"I see. Are we now exempt from the threads of fate?"

Zacharias falls silent for a few moments. "Only time will tell."

Zacharias hands me the dead sea creature, coated with chunky jelly. The charred fish harbors little to no taste. Soterios and I have no right to refuse. Beggars can't be choosers.

I wonder why Fate dished out such awful culinary skills to this already lonesome forest-dweller. Travelers definitely aren't flocking to him for food. I understand why Avi was so quick to turn back. Not to mention, anything that comes out of Zacharias' mouth is either an insult, an awful pun, or an off-the-wall construct. He would get along well with the older folks in my family that love nothing more than telling stories of their youth and lecturing their one grandchild, me, about how I'm ruining my life by not living it to its fullest. I developed the ability to tune them out years ago. After sitting a while with Zacharias and his musings regarding Fate, I wonder if they do have something of value to offer after all.

The sun goes down, but we fail to notice. Located so far from the cave's mouth and artificially lit during the day, the makeshift home functions on an entirely different schedule. My body, however, tells me that it's time to sleep, even as Zacharias still shuffles about. He senses us growing weary and tells us to rest and prepare for tomorrow. He promises that he'll help us face our curses, but not in the way we initially had our hearts set on.

Before he goes off to bed, I ask, "Why did I see the soldier and the girl? Who are they? Why would Fate show them to me?"

"Maybe you're destined to meet. But I can't help but feel like they hold great importance to this world. If our story has been foretold, they may be the protagonist and deuteragonist." He chuckles to himself.

It's a miracle that I managed to fall asleep on a heap of woolen blankets and half-stuffed pillows. My mind was brimming with

questions and concerns. I wake up to Zacharias' foot driving into my stomach. I scream. Try being woken up by a kick to the ribs, see how that feels. He then hands me a mug of tea. A little baffled by this morning ritual, I accept the beverage. Inside the mug, I find a green liquid with little leaves floating on the surface, sending tiny ripples across the tea. I take a seat on yesterday's cushioned stool. Soterios is already awake, sitting in an armchair. He also grips a mug tightly with both hands, one around the side, the other curled around the handle. Red residue lingers on his lips.

"When you're done, come find me outside," Zacharias calls out as he ducks through the fairy door. Sometimes I'm grateful that I'm not very tall. Being shorter than Soterios always embarrassed me, but at least I don't have a bouquet of lanky, awkward limbs like Zacharias. People often speculate about a correlation between height and belligerence. The shorter the stature, the greater the rage. In the past, this has undeniably applied to me.

"Blood?" I reluctantly ask.

Soterios stares into his mug and gives me a small nod. He sets it down on a coffee table. Soterios changes the subject, avoiding eye contact with me. "I think this place needs some redecorating,"

I look around.

Yes, he does.

Zacharias' furnishings are a conglomeration of antiques that were seemingly thrown out by others and put to use by him. Nothing has the same pattern or colors. Even our mugs are various shapes, colors, and sizes, as if they were made in different eras. If each item had a little price tag, this place would be the perfect pawn

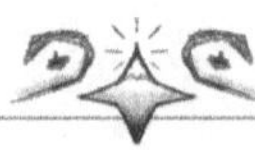

shop. A framed photograph on a cluttered bookshelf catches my eye. The glass has a few cracks in it, but not enough to obstruct my vision from the subjects of the photograph. I narrow my focus to make out their identities. Avi, without his cloak, stands smiling next to Zacharias. Zacharias' manic smirk looks familiar. Strikingly, however, he is missing his extra set of arms. I can't imagine when this photograph would have been taken, and under what circumstances.

We find Zacharias outside with several handfuls of berries. This locally-sourced breakfast isn't a suitable meal, but at least it's better than what we ate last night. He leads us on a walk through the woods, but orders us to remain silent. I assume the hike will be the first step on our path to redemption.

"Be quiet. Don't think too much about what you're looking at. Instead, pay attention to how you *feel*," Zacharias commands the both of us.

As we venture further from the cave, the mixture of trees fades into a wooded area composed of only slender pine trees. Each tree is spaced approximately a yard away from the next, creating an eerie grid of perfectly positioned pines. Our crunching footsteps fade into nothingness on the padded amber needles of the forest floor. The towering trees creak as the wind sways them from side to side with each and every gust. The subtle noise grants the silent forest a hair-raising aura. I dare not speak, yet still have the urge to ask if anyone else feels the same way. I suppress my words and fright with a gulp. Such freakish perfection seems like it should not be disturbed, yet here this path winds and weaves through the flawless trees. Something about these woods reminds me of Zacharias. What? I can't quite place my finger on it. Maybe he is a speck of imperfection in a seemingly flawless existence crafted by Fate. Maybe he *is* the perfection and we all strive to be as in-tune with the natural world. I stare up at the towering pines in search of answers, as if the light peeking through the branches and needles could provide me with a reply.

Is Fate truly responsible for determining every detail of our lives, from the creaking branches above, to the way the wind blows through my hair, down to each passing breath? Similar to an author or artist, whose pen and paper produce worlds of works. A moment, a scene, a world, crafted to perfection in their mind. Or maybe even perfectly warped, riddled with purposeful flaws. Just as I fail to understand the thought process of an artist, I fall short of grasping the concept of Fate's divine composition.

This is too much for me to fathom at this point in time. Instead of grasping the abstract concept, I focus on the details of the present. Without his lenses, a sheer glare no longer comes off of Soterios' glasses, allowing me to see his eyes. His pupils dart from one swaying tree to the next. Has he never seen the world clearly without lenses before? My guess is as good as anyone else's, minus his. Zacharias keeps an eye on us by spontaneously checking over his shoulder. Sometimes, he'll give us a quick glance. At other times, he'll stare. His light irises almost blend in with the whites of his eyes. Small flecks of various pastel colors remind me of shimmering opals. Soterios' newly ruby irises attract attention, wanted or not. If only I had fascinating features, as well. My eyes are plain, too simple, just brown. Yep. Brown. The most common eye color in the world.

My mind wanders off again, somewhere beyond this abyss of rasping trees, and I once more lose sight of our goal here. To feel, right? As much as I did not want to feel the hair-raising aura of the woods, something tells me that my future wobbles on the line, depending on my decisions here and now. The dried pine needles squish under my boots, sinking ever so slightly with each footstep. A few needles soaked with sap tag along, clinging to the treads of my shoes. The air smells of pine and brisk cold. The insides of my nostrils almost sting from the dry autumn air. My senses are alive. Even when I'm miles away from everything I know, I feel at home here, amongst the tawny hues. Maybe there's something to be appreciated in the color of my brown eyes. Fate put me in this space for a deliberate purpose.

Is this Zacharias' unspoken tenet?

When the cave comes back in sight, Zacharias instructs me to sit on a rock. I follow his orders. A small pond surrounds the large stone. When I say small, I mean tiny. Someone can't even swim in it. I slip my boots off despite the cool weather, wade through the shallow water, and crawl onto the large rock that sits in the middle. The moss tickles my bare feet, creeping into the crevasses between my chilly toes. My eyes close. The leaves rustle around me. Soterios sits a few yards away, reading his book. The pages of the novel flap every so often. I feel Zacharias' intense stare from behind.

"Embrace the collective, serene emotionality of nature through your physicality," he whispers.

"*Eh!?*"

My cheek twitches and my brain tweeks. I have no idea what he means by that, so I do my best to comply. He tells me to be calm, yet I always feel at odds in his presence. His actions are too irrational and spontaneous for me to lower my guard.

My muscles grow tense with concern as I realize that Zacharias now stands in the ankle-deep water before me. Small fish swim around his feet, remarkably unbothered.

"Don't you know anything about meditation?" Zacharias taps my nose. Cross-eyed, I stare at his finger. "Ah, you're doing the opposite of what you need to. Your form is crooked."

"Huh? Whatever you say!"

Begrudgingly, I shut my eyes and straighten my spine. I suck my lips in, hoping that my formation is now correct.

"You're too stiff. Loosen up."

My chin instinctively dips down to nod. Even when I try my best to relax, I still can't shake off the two pairs of eyes that are fixated on me. Zacharias' disappointment does not fade. He sighs. "You understand the point of this, right?"

I shake my head.

At least I think I do.

A groan soon follows. "You and your friend are cursed, charmed. They're intrinsically synonymous. A divine being has given you the power to fine-tune your synergy with the world around you. Notice that as I move about this pond, the fish accept my presence. Blend, don't blunder." He goes on to add, "Julius, you failed to see what was right in front of you and the potential of your curse. You lived your life shallow and blind. You panicked when you lost your vision in the forest, but it opened up your world to deeper comprehension of yourself and those around you. This extraordinary perception of Fate's scriptures enables you to slip into the consciousness of others, exposing yourself to their

emotions, thoughts, and outlooks on life. The true definition of empathy."

I reflect on the past few days. The places we've been. The people we've met. James. Reo. Vylad. Derek. Astoria. Avi. Zacharias. Each offered their own gifts and talents to unconditionally aid our journey. Before, I would have taken these amenities for granted, but now I feel newfound appreciation and gratitude.

Zacharias continues, now addressing Soterios, "As for you, lovely lad. You were simply helpless, bound to the knowledge you once gained from books. Literature has value, but there's more to experiencing the fullness of life. You get hurt, you get back up. Vampires are resilient beings, facing both the dangers of pride and prejudice. You've already started to embrace your race. You must not drown in self-pity, but use this curse as a lifeboat to stay afloat and face the waves ahead."

I glance over my shoulder at my friend. He stares up from his closed book. Beneath his lensless frames, I recognize bittersweet surrender in his watery eyes.

"To me," Zacharias drives home his point as he gazes down at the tranquil fish, "the world becomes more beautiful when you liberate your mind. You begin to appreciate the little things in life that Fate has created."

The next morning, I wake up on my own. Soterios sits in another chair, still fast asleep. Observing his tranquil slumber, it dawns upon me that Soterios is so much stronger than I am. He always has been. I didn't hate him because I disliked his personality. I shunned him because I wanted to be him. Yes, he was physically and socially weak. He couldn't run. He couldn't hold his own in battle. He couldn't even start a conversation. Still, he hid his vulnerability. He never let emotions, ridicule, or pain dull his rationality. He's a problem solver by nature. I, on the other hand, am a problem causer. I'm lucky to have him as a foil.

Careful not to wake Soterios, I creep out of the fairy door and weave my way through the stalagmites and stalactites. I exit the cave through the veil of vines. Zacharias has his back to me and tends his fire with a twig. Today, he has two arms, rather than four, like in the photograph of Avi and him. Instead of a witty greeting or snarky remark, a sniffle comes from his direction. I walk up behind him, keeping my hands behind my back with my fingers knitted together. Zacharias continues to stare at the sky with glossy eyes and tear-stained cheeks. His lips subtly quiver in front of his bared teeth as he grieves. If he had been alone, the rustling of the autumn leaves and rush of the creek would have concealed his cries from the rest of the world. Oblivious to the source of his evident pain, I quietly sit down next to him.

"I don't know if it was a good thing that Fate brought you here," he admits, rolling his head over to face me.

"Are you upset that we're here? We can leave if you want us to," I offer, a little confused by his uncharacteristic change of heart.

"Oh shush, you big lummox. Your predicament has brought back so many awful memories, reminding me of how charms really are curses in a way," Zacharias rolls his eyes before looking away. "What a pain, how every coin has two sides. Just like Fate herself. When she wants something accomplished, the whole world gathers to achieve that goal. Is it a beautiful masterpiece or a heinous tragedy? Is she a creator or an annihilator?"

"You're harmless, I can't imagine why she would want you dead."

"I wasn't meant to live in this era. My time should have come and gone hundreds of years ago. She's afraid of me messing up her pretty pictures. My curse has granted me immortality, but she can end my existence with the flick of a pen. Even with that option at her disposal, she proceeds to make aspects of my life a living nightmare. She made me a *monster*. Because of her, everyone I grow attached to eventually leaves me, so I strive to isolate myself from impending betrayal." As he speaks, his tone fades from melancholy, to annoyance, and finally to rage.

"Is that why Avi didn't want to return? You were smiling in that photograph, but he didn't want anything to do with you during our last encounter."

Zacharias sighs, letting off some steam. "You could say that. He was another student of mine, such a fine spellcaster, but unwilling to take his skills to the next level. He left to start his own legacy protecting the persecuted folk of this kingdom. I begged for him to stay, but now he just thinks that I'm a maniac." Zacharias explained, but soon admits, "He's not wrong. My heart aches a little bit to think that he sees me as a four-armed beast like everyone else."

"Then why don't you present yourself like *this*?" I gesture to his two arms. Other than his mysterious mahogany skin and white hair, he kind of looks like a normal man now.

"After a while, I stopped caring. There's no point in trying to be anything other than a monster if everyone else is set on believing that I am. Besides, using magic to give myself an extra pair of arms is quite convenient."

"Well," I begin, trying to match his level of profoundness, "you don't have to think that way. Like you told Soterios, prejudice is only another trial that you face on the road to self-improvement. I bet that you can prove people wrong. If not now, then one day."

After rubbing the glossy film out of his eyes, Zacharias merely smiles at me. He stands, overlooking the small pond filled with gently rippling water and docile fish. Though, I come to find that his reflection in the water is not his own. A white-haired boy with circular glasses gazes back up at him. The boy's serene smile matches Zacharias' current expression. I never realized how sentimental 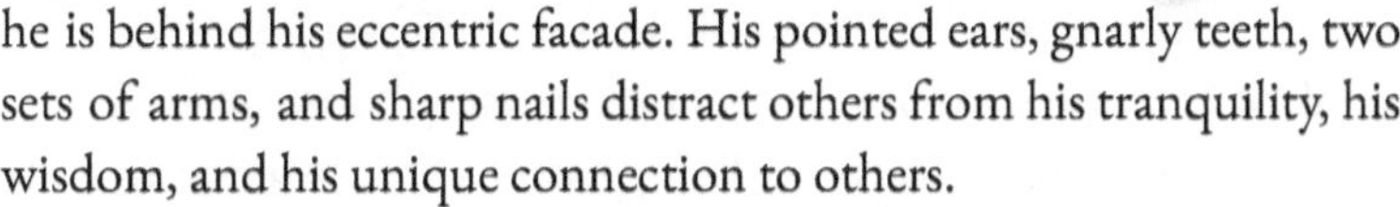 he is behind his eccentric facade. His pointed ears, gnarly teeth, two sets of arms, and sharp nails distract others from his tranquility, his wisdom, and his unique connection to others.

"Thanks." He faces me once more. "I'll gladly wait for that day to come. In the meantime, you've still got a lot of growing to do. This should give you a solid foundation to work with. I believe that you and your friend are ready to face the real world. Bring that little fashionable business twerp in next. I'll set 'em right."

I laugh a little bit. Reo needs guidance and a big shove off of his self-proclaimed almighty throne. This isn't about him. A wave of relief comes over me as I let out a grand sigh. Even though Zacharias thinks I'm ready, I'm not sure if I'm prepared to face my parents. My brewing homesickness, however, pushes me to wake Soterios. He must be feeling the same way. We've been gone for too

long. Our clothes are dirty, we're bloodstained, and we're bruised. In defiance, he grumbles under his breath before rolling over. I tell him about our plan to return to my home in Vertrauville. I drag him through the fairy door and outside the cave. Using his hand as a visor, he squints at the morning light.

"Are you a vampire or something?" Zacharias snickers.

Soterios raises a brow at the joke at first, then catches on and nods. "You could say that."

Once we're prepared to part ways, Zacharias sets a tiny, golden jingle bell in each of our palms. They match Avi's. Apparently all of Zacharias' students receive one.

As I examine the bell, I can't help but think of Christmas. Merry carols sing alongside the jingling of bells for the holiday season. Are these for an early Celebration? After all, we're approaching December, yet still a couple months off. Zacharias almost knows what I'm thinking.

"For good luck and warding off bad vibes. Of course, along with proof that you were my apprentices."

He also hands Soterios a pouch of coins. By its weight, I assume that there's enough money to get us two train tickets and a few meals on our way home. His generous gifts won't be taken for granted. Zacharias waves us off from the mouth of his cave. The flowering vines cast a shadow over his already dark skin, though his opal eyes and smile shine. He wishes us safe travels with hopes of our paths crossing again. We set off. This time, homebound.

Chapter 7:
The Return

Once again, we cross paths with the purple trail on our way to Avi's camp. Astoria waves and smiles as we approach. Soterios thanks Avi for his guidance, so I follow his lead and express my gratitude as well. Avi looks bewildered to see us again. Today, he's holding his staff like a walking stick, instead of carrying it over his shoulder. He looks too young and able-bodied to be holding a cane.

"Did you not expect us to come back?" I raise a brow.

"No. I thought you would take longer. Zacharias kept me there for years," he claims as he flicks the bell on his ear in frustration. He requests our pardon before disappearing into one of the floral huts. Astoria tags along with him.

"What do you think he's doing?" I lean over Soterios' shoulder. He shrugs.

After a minute or two, Avi returns with a neatly wrapped gift topped with a makeshift ribbon made out of long strands of grass. "You have my delayed thanks for safely returning Astoria from the festival. I am guilty of breaking my personal codes by going into town as well. I'm assuming you understand the fear of losing family members and companions. Humans are too scared of what they don't understand."

As he offloads the box into my arms, I ask, "What is it?"

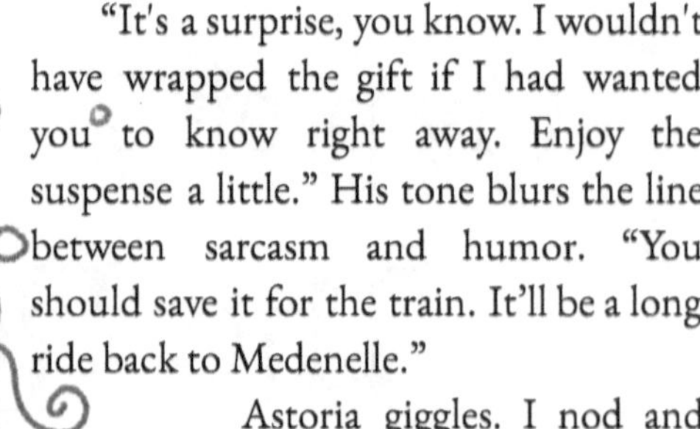

"It's a surprise, you know. I wouldn't have wrapped the gift if I had wanted you to know right away. Enjoy the suspense a little." His tone blurs the line between sarcasm and humor. "You should save it for the train. It'll be a long ride back to Medenelle."

Astoria giggles. I nod and hand the package off to Soterios.

"It's time you head home, no?" Avi shifts his staff from one hand to the other. His eyebrows frown as his eyes glisten with a sense of gloom. Even his jackal ears slightly flatten in woe.

The fear of losing family members and companions. I think back to what he said before. He must be concerned for our families. Soterios' lips curl into a small smile.

"Yes."

We say our last goodbyes to the woodland folk before setting off to pass back through Milledale's capital city. The golden leaves tumble on their way to the forest floor. Some crunch under my boots, while others flutter to the side as I kick them out of the way. I'm still a child in some ways. Even though my mind and body have matured, I still make silly decisions, more often than not. I miss the wonder and flamboyant creativity of my younger self, but now I know better than to run off and put others in danger.

Soterios isn't very chatty as we approach the village, but I'm used to his tendencies. He still has a lot to process and accept, but even more to explain. If he gets expelled, it'll all be my fault. There's no way I could ever make that sort of loss up to him. School and knowledge define him; they're engraved into his core. Without that, he's just another unfortunate teenager.

Drunk townsfolk, hungover from the festival, stumble about the streets, where other inhabitants are cleaning up. The elven mother we saw on our first trip through Milledale watches her red-headed boy run amuck in the street with other children. I wonder how she avoids being discovered by the knights. I find it hard to imagine what it's like growing up in the middle of a city, rather than on a secluded ranch. I wonder what it's like to live entirely in the Mirror Realm, without knowledge of phones, cars, and televisions kept blindly yet content in the dark, unknowingly living the life of a fairytale character. My mind teems with newfound curiosity, empathy, and clarity.

We make our way down the muddy trail to Pericuton to catch the sunset train. I witness the breathtaking architecture of the station, the high cathedral ceilings adorned with chipping paintings. The cracks in the wall add to the old building's antique beauty. Using almost all of Zacharias' money, we purchase our tickets. The train rolls in soon after, bringing in clouds of steam.

Once we take our seats, Soterios opens up to me. We chat the whole ride home. We discuss our adventure but don't dwell too much on the past. I find his fangs easier to look at, easier to accept. Our withering tolerance has blossomed into a flourishing friendship.

As our conversation lulls, we agree on opening Avi's gift. Soterios pulls on the grass ribbon, unraveling the bow. He slowly unwraps the gift to reveal a brown box. Taking initiative, I reach over and open the box. Two bundles of wooden sticks tied together and two glass bottles full of a light purple liquid slide out. Like the gift's packaging, grass bows are tied neatly around the bottles and sticks in order to group them together. I glance at Soterios in hopes of him knowing what exactly the gift is.

Of course, he has the answer. "It's a reed diffuser. Zacharias used them for meditation, if I recall correctly."

"How'd you know what it is?"

"He had one in his bookcase. My mother used to buy them for me. I'd use peppermint oils for studying. She told me it helps with focus, but each one has a different effect."

"Oh, so we'll be able to meditate on our own now!"

Soterios nods. "Avi must have learned how to use them during his tutelage under Zacharias."

I pop off the cork of one bottle and inhale. I don't recognize the smell.

"By its color, I'm guessing it's lavender," Soterios examines his bottle. "It'll be good for calming your senses."

I recall the overwhelming visions I saw last train ride and our experiences in the forest. Sometimes situations are too much for one to handle on one's own. I'm glad that Soterios stuck with me to the end, even though I put him in danger over and over again. As I rub the back of my neck, my eyebrows draw together.

"All of this is all my fault," I admit. "Back there, in my room, you told me that running away was a poor idea. I should have listened to you."

"It's okay. If I were you I wouldn't have listened either," Soterios tells me. "I never respected you, but I do now. I always wanted to be your friend, but I convinced myself you were too reckless to stay by my side."

"That's not wrong." I awkwardly smile, fidgeting with the cuff of my sleeve.

Soterios' gaze lingers past the horizon, maybe somewhere beyond this realm, but before the next. His reflection stays beside him, even as the rolling hills and looming forests pass by.

"But that's different now," he mumbles as his red eyes glance up at me, "right?"

Caught a little off guard, I pause for a moment with my own wide eyes. "Yes. You're right."

The person I was a week ago would have never admitted such things. If Soterios stated that two plus two equals four, I would have declared that it added up to anything *but* four. Now, I find myself valuing what he has to say, even counting on him.

I shut my eyes and allow myself to escape from the present, into the future. I see Soterios sitting at a desk in front of a stack of papers, surrounded by curious individuals dressed in formal attire. A bookshelf, full of what I assumed to be textbooks and records, towers behind them. The group smiles and laughs. A blinding light flashes as a girl snaps a picture. The image prints out of the top. The amateur photographer shakes the newly born image and pins it among a corkboard of others. Another vision takes this one's place and I see myself with a formal collared shirt and sweater. The embroidered crest of Mark Bruik's school rests on my chest. I turn around to find the horned boy I'd seen in my earlier dreams staring

at me with a heartfelt smile. He looks a few years older than before. He thanks me, but I don't know what for. I open my eyes and process the divination. I see hope for Soterios' future, as well as direction for my own. Whatever lies on the road ahead, I will bid welcome to Fate's wishes when the time comes.

I see the sunset through the train's window with new eyes and a fresh mind. Purple and pink values merge as the sun pulls the warm orange and yellow hues out of the sky. The navy blue of twilight brings darkness upon the still cornfields. The night sky reminds me of Zacharias, the crescent moon and speckled stars resembling his smile and freckles. I doze off to the repetitive rattling of the rails.

The station approaches quickly as the sun rises. It strikes me that the time it takes to return home always feels far shorter than the time it takes to go somewhere new. We visit our former travel companions, James and Reo, at the pharmacy as we pass through Medenelle. James greets us with a relieved wave from behind the counter. Reo, in true character, immediately complains that we took longer than he expected, as he is scheduled to return to the Overworld the following day. Beneath his rant, I'm sure he's glad he gets to see us one last time before returning to the bustling streets of New York City.

"You don't have the blindfold anymore." James notes, raising his brows. "Your vision has been restored?"

I nod. He smiles in return. "I'm glad."

"Oh, come on. Julius gives off big protagonist vibes, so of course he's okay! Right!?" Reo exclaims.

"You nerd." I roll my eyes.

Soterios laughs a little.

"It's good to see you two together again. Unlikely friends sometimes make the best friends," James tells us, giving Reo a hearty pat on the back.

We take a winding dirt road, avoiding the woods on our way back to Vertrauville.

Coming home. My favorite feeling.

Whether it's from school, from a vacation, or from running away, my home's welcoming embrace always feels the same.

As my house comes back in sight, we sprint towards it. I don't know how we'll be received, but I know that Soterios will stay by my side through it all. And just how do I know that? The patchwork of our improbable friendship has been sewn together by the threads of amends.

Acknowledgements & Artwork

After intense calculations, I have concluded that Threads of Amends takes place the year I was born. 2006? *Yikes*, oh dear, how long ago was that? 16 years? Soon to be far, far more. Bring forth my cane as I become Julius' grandparents who tell stories beginning with "when I was a lad..." Y'know a lot has changed, haha. Once upon a time, we read books on paper. Yes, paper. Now we're encouraged to read books online. No thanks. I'd rather dump my money into pricey hardcovers and paperbacks than hunch over a screen called an "eBook." My friends, family, and wallet can vouch for me.

But, hey, to each their own. Not everyone smells books and goes, "*Hmmm*, yes. Me likey."

But do I?

Yes.

Did we pass a book around my college-level AP Language and Composition course for scent-related purposes?

Also yes.

Cheers to the little things, and totally this book. Through Zacharias, I wanted to express how young people take everything they see for granted, and how students, *especially* 'honors kids,' seek to rush and complete work as fast as possible, rather than understanding and cherishing the process. I'm guilty of those actions. Sometimes, you don't have to try. The world just absorbs you. As a girl who plays by monkey-see monkey-do, I find myself standing, kneeling, and sitting in front of my family's ever-growing bookshelf in search of guidance and inspiration for my own books. Each novel carries its own story, but also some sort of attachment. Bookmarks from previous attempts to finish a volume slide out, falling to the ground. I learned my father's habits of using dust jackets as bookmarks when pulling out his political novels. Little, nearly incomprehensible cursive notes from relatives greet those who crack open the covers of well-picked gifts. And of course, the urge to decipher foreign languages comes hand-in-hand with French copies of Narnia, having five years of learning French under your belt. Memories flood back, reminding me of a simpler time when my father would read to my brother and me in the evenings. The moments of us huddled on either side of my father, eager to find out what happens next in historical fiction had escaped my mind until I held that secret book in my hands.

To me, you don't always have to write a compelling story to have an impactful novel. A little aspect just needs to make it stand out, and that task is not always yours. One book stood out to me due to it repeating its title five times before the book actually began. I remember some books because of their astounding covers. Some books are cherishable gifts. Beautifully written books that make us cry leave permanent tear-stains on our heart. We're the ones who determine the value and stories behind stories that make these paper sandwiches so delicious.

(Disclaimer: No, I am *not* encouraging you to eat paper.)

A huge thank you and a giant shoutout to all of the people who have read and supported *Matthew Eversen and the Wild Space Goose Chase*, my first book! I've definitely come a long way since then in terms of writing, art, and format design, so I hope you all enjoy this simple story! The thought behind this book was to introduce Julius' backstory, whose name was subtly referenced in *Matthew Eversen and the Wild Space Goose Chase*! If you look close

enough, you'll find him in there. Even though *Matthew Eversen* is a trilogy, I still wanted to complete this story before I moved on to write the second volume. Don't worry, the sequels are in the works! Maybe more characters from this book will appear in Matthew's extra-terrestrial adventure. (Hint, hint!)

In addition to refining my book design and writing skills, I wanted to classify this book as a "bite-sized fantasy novella," after reading a myriad of short, yet impactful novels. These included *Of Mice and Men*, *No Longer Human*, *The Setting Sun*, *The Alchemist*, and *The Stranger*.

(Yes, I'm *obsessed* with classical literature!)

I've found longer books more difficult to stick with, especially when I'm involved with extracurricular activities, difficult classes, creative hobbies, and projects, like this book. Time just vanishes! (Sir Isaac Newton claims that matter and energy can neither be created nor destroyed, but he doesn't include time, *muhaha*!) Many others find themselves longing to read, but lacking enough time to finish. In hopes of accomplishing what these short, but sweet, books have done, I kept Threads of Amends a little over thirty-thousand words, including this side note.

Of course, I'd love to thank my mother for her continuous accompaniment in my strange endeavors and for being my favorite emotional support human. I'd like to thank my brother, despite his brutal comments and interjections, for helping me create the little train on the cover and decide on the title color. I'd like to thank my dad for, y'know, moral support from the couch.

Shoutout to everyone who helped sway my decisions for this book, such as character art, fonts, chapter headers, etc. along with people who have given feedback on the artwork, characters, and plot. Kudos to the lovely editor, my mother, who is not afraid to tell me that a sentence sounds stupid. Thanks to Mrs. Goodwin, my 7th grade English teacher, who inspired me to write! Lastly, thank you to everyone who supports my writing by giving me smiles, feedback, and our course buying copies! Seeing my book in someone else's hands brings me happiness that words cannot begin to describe. (Ironic since I'm supposed to be good with words as an author...)

One last thing! I was super excited to go through and illustrate items and characters who pop up throughout the book, rather than just characters at the end. (Like in *Matthew Eversen and the Wild Space Goose Chase*! We'll get an illustrated edition one day!)

Other than the *Matthew Eversen* trilogy, I've been working on other projects, such as *Apthnorath*, a death game novel, and *Trailblazer*, the story of the horned-boy from Julius' visions! (It's also the book that *Threads of Amends* foreshadows and parallels!)

Personally, my favorite artwork is the perfect sandwich in Chapter 5: The Guide. Of course, I absolutely adore designing characters, so in addition to the chapter illustrations, I simply had to include artwork of Julius, Soterios, Reo, and James in the back of this book! I hope you love them as much as I do!

Julius Subedar

Soterios Solace

Reo Akabane

James
Thomas

About the Author

Mia Dorsch is an artistic author. Dreaming of whimsical lands, she brings out-of-this-world ideas to life. You can find her spending her days with earbuds plugged in and lost to lyrics as she navigates fantastical realms. When she's not daydreaming with music, you can find her behind the circulation desk at Lewes Public Library or curled up somewhere, pen or book in-hand. Here, she's playing hooky with her brother, A.K.A. her awesome photographer! *The Alchemist, the Siren, and the Thief* is her third novel, but *Threads of Amends* will always have a special little spot in her heart.

More Books by Mia

Matthew Eversen and the Wild Space Goose Chase

Czar: Testimony No. 1

The Alchemist, the Siren, & the Thief

* 9 7 9 8 9 9 9 1 6 8 8 6 3 5 *